Thirty-Three Teeth

ALSO BY COLIN COTTERILL

The Coroner's Lunch
Disco for the Departed

Thirty-Three Teeth

COLIN COTTERILL

VINTAGE CANADA

VINTAGE CANADA EDITION, 2006

Copyright © 2005 Colin Cotterill

Published in Canada by Vintage Canada, a division of Random House
of Canada Limited, Toronto, in 2006. Originally published by Soho
Press Inc., New York, in the United States of America in 2005.
Distributed by Random House of Canada Limited, Toronto.

Vintage Canada and colophon are registered trademarks of
Random House of Canada Limited.

www.randomhouse.ca

Library and Archives Canada Cataloguing in Publication

Cotterill, Colin
Thirty-three teeth / Colin Cotterill.

(A Dr. Siri Paiboun mystery)
ISBN-13: 978-0-676-97832-2
ISBN-10: 0-676-97832-0

I. Title. II. Series: Cotterill, Colin. Dr. Siri Paiboun mystery.

PR6053.O7775T45 2006   823'.92   C2006-901079-X

Text design: Kathleen Lake, Neuwirth and Associates

Printed and bound in Canada

2 4 6 8 9 7 5 3 1

With love to my family for all their years of faith and support.

Contents

The neon hammer and sickle buzzed and flickered into life over the night club of the Lan Xang Hotel. The sun had plummeted mauvely into Thailand across the Mekhong River, and the hotel waitresses were lighting the little lamps that turned the simple sky-blue room into a mysterious nighttime cavern.

In an hour, a large Vietnamese delegation would be offered diversion there by members of the Lao People's Revolutionary Party Politburo. They'd be made to watch poor country boys in fur hats do a Lao falling-over version of cossack dancing. They'd be forced to suck semi-fermented rice whiskey from large tubs through long straws until they were dizzy. They'd finally be coerced into embarrassing dances with solid girls in ankle-length skirts and crusty makeup.

And, assuming they survived these delights, they'd be allowed to return to their rooms to sleep. Next day, with heads heavy as pressed rubber, they'd sign their names to documents laying the foundations for the forthcoming Lao/Vietnam Treaty of Friendship, and they probably wouldn't remember very much about it.

But that was all to come. The understaffed hotel day shift had been replaced by an understaffed night crew. The sweating receptionist was ironing a shirt in the glass office behind her desk. The chambermaid was running a bowl of rice porridge up to a sick guest on the third floor.

Outside, an old guard, in a jacket so large it reached his knees, was locking the back gate that opened onto Sethathirat Road. At night, the gate kept out dogs and the occasional traveler tempted to come into the garden in search of respite from the cruel hot-season nights. An eight-foot wall protected the place as if it were something more special than it was.

Leaves floated in a greasy swimming pool. Obedient flowers stood in well-spaced regiments, better watered than any of the households outside along the street. And then there were the cages. They were solid concrete, so squat that a tall man would have to stoop to see inside. Two were empty. They housed only the spirits of animals temporarily imprisoned there: a monkey replaced by a deer, a peacock taking over the sentence of a wild dog.

But in the grim shadows of the third cage, something wheezed. It moved seldom, only to scratch lethargically at its dry skin. The unchristened black mountain bear was hosed down along with the bougainvilleas and given scraps from the kitchen from time to time. Its fur was patchy and dull, like a carpet in a well-trodden passage. Buddha only knew how the creature had survived for so long in its cramped jail, and the Lord had been banished from the socialist republic some fifteen months hence.

People came in the early evening and at weekends to stand in front of the cage and stare at her. She stared back, although her glazed bloodshot eyes could no longer make out details of the mocking faces. Children laughed and pointed. Brave fathers poked sticks in through the bars, but the black mountain bear no longer appeared to give a damn.

They naturally blamed the old guard the next day. "Too much rice whiskey," they said. "Slack," they said. The guard denied it, of course. He swore he'd relocked the cage door. He'd thrown the leftovers from the Vietnamese banquet into the animal's bowl and locked the cage. He was sure of it. He swore the beast was still in there when he did his rounds at four. He swore he had no idea how it could have gotten out, or where it could have gone. But they sacked him anyway.

After a panicked search of the grounds and the hotel buildings, the manager declared to his staff that the place was safe and it was a problem now for the police. In fact, he didn't think it would be wise to mention the escape to his guests at all. As far as he was concerned, the problem was over.

But for Vientiane, it had barely started.

Tomb Sweet Tomb

The sun baked everything in the new suburb. Comrade Civilai stepped from the hot black limousine and, without locking the doors, walked up to the concrete mausoleum where they'd put Dr. Siri. The gate and the front door were open, and he could see clear through to the small yard at the back. There was no furniture to interrupt the view.

He kicked off his Sunday sandals and walked into the front room. It was as if the builders and decorators had just left. The walls were still virgin Wattay light-blue, to match the swimming-pool-colored Wattay airport. They were unencumbered by pictures or posters or photographs of heroes of the revolution. No French plaster ducks flew in formation. No clock ticked. If he didn't know Siri had lived here for a month, he would have guessed this to be a vacant house.

On his way to the back, he passed a small room where piles of clothes told him he was nearing a primitive life form. In the back yard, he discovered it. Dr. Siri Paiboun, reluctant national coroner, confused psychic, disheartened communist, swung gently on a hammock strung between two jackfruit saplings. A larger man would have brought them both down.

In his shadow, Saloop, rescued street dog and lifesaver, drooled onto the hot earth. He looked up with one eye, decided Civilai was too old and bald to be a threat, and returned to his dream.

A month earlier, the yard had been dirt and debris. Today it was a jungle. Siri had gone to great pains to recreate the environment in which he'd spent the latter forty of his seventy-two years. For the past four weekends, he and his trusted morgue colleagues had set off into the outer suburbs and denuded them unashamedly. They'd transported a variety of trees and shrubs back to this humble bunker—the Party's thanks for his services.

"I do hope I'm not disturbing you," Civilai said, knowing full well how disturbing he was being. Siri's eerie green eyes opened slowly to see his best friend leaning over him.

"Ah, boy. Just put the iced lime juice on the table there and get back to the servants' quarters post-haste."

Civilai was two days older than the doctor. Both born in the year of the rabbit, they showed its characteristic industry and guile. Yet neither had exhibited its lustiness: they'd married their first loves and been totally faithful. They were of a rare breed of rabbit in Laos.

"So, this is how the bourgeois medical profession spends its Sundays. Shouldn't you be out digging ditches for the republic?" He sat back on the wooden cot on the small veranda.

"I'm a frail old man, brother. A day of physical labor could very well put me on the slab. I doubt I have a month left to live as it is. That's why your politburo buddies should be searching high and low for a coroner to replace me now."

There was nothing frail about Dr. Siri. He was so far from the black archers of death, he wouldn't be hearing their arrows thumping into the dry earth for many years to come. His short, solid body still scurried hither and thither like a curious river rat. Younger men were hard-pressed to keep his pace.

His mind, resplendent with its newly honed skills, had become even keener of late. He'd always been a logical man; but in the last five months, he'd acquired the type of knowledge that isn't given out in universities. For reasons he was still trying to fathom, he'd been delegated Laos's honorary consul to the spirit world.

This new posting proved ideally suited to his job as the head and only coroner of the Lao People's Democratic Republic. He still hadn't been able to control the visits from his spirit clients or find a way to ask specific questions of them, but they came to him regularly with clues. What he lacked in experience (he'd only been a coroner for a year), he could often make up for by communing with the dead. His three-dimensional mind had acquired a fourth dimension.

"You know we could never replace you, little brother. You're a legend," Civilai replied.

"A legend?" Siri slid up the hammock to a sitting position. "Isn't a legend something that's long-winded and not widely believed?"

"You've got it."

"Hot, isn't it?"

"Damned hot."

This was the hot-season anthem that could be heard *ad infinitum* around the capital. It had been a particularly hot year so far, so it got even more repetition than usual.

For the first time, Siri noticed the cloth bag that Civilai held on his lap. "You bring me something?"

"Nothing you'd be interested in."

"Let me be the judge of that."

"The Soviets have been courting us. They want permission to build a satellite dish to spy on the Yanks. While we think about it, they pepper us with these little incentives." He teased the cap of a bottle from his bag.

"Vodka?"

"Moskovskaya; best you can get. But I don't suppose you're thirsty."

Siri was off the hammock and rattling around in the kitchen for a second glass before the word *thirsty* had left Civilai's lips.

The late morning had become late afternoon.

"I don't know how the Russians can strink-this-duff." Civilai's slurring turned the comment into one long word.

"Me, too. No wonder the women are hairier than the women."

"Men."

"Where?"

So had the conversation deteriorated. There were two modest glassfuls left in the bottom of the bottle. The friends sat side by side on the long, uncomfortable wooden cot. The garden wasn't moving at all, but they swayed like survivors in a lifeboat. Civilai looked up at a rolled mosquito net tied above their heads.

"You sleep out here, Li'l Brother?"

Siri shook his head from side to side. "Yes."

"What's the point of having a house?"

"That's it. That's the very something I asked Judge Haeng. But he wouldn't let me have the garden without it. He said"—Siri put on the whiny high-pitched accent of his young superior— "'We are senior members of the party, Comrade Siri. As such, we have to lead by example. Sleeping in trees should remain the exclusive domain of the primates.' I was surprised he knew what a primate was."

"What have you got against houses?"

"Houses I have not a nothing against. But this isn't a house. A house is an airy wooden thing on slits that—"

"Stilts."

"I said that. On slits, that creaks when you walk around. It sways in heavy winds and leaks in the rainy season. This? This is a sarcahoph . . . a . . . a saroph . . . sarpho . . . sarcophagus."

"Well said."

"What is this regime's fixation on concrete?"

"Sustainability. This house will still be here in a thousand years, after ten generations of your wooden houses have fallen down. Remember the three little pigs."

"That's it. It's a sty."

"It's not."

"Then it's a tomb. I feel entombed. It's so morbid in there."

"How can you, of all people, complain about morbidity?"

"I'm a coroner. Not a corpse."

Civilai laughed and leaned back against the wall. "How are your ghostly friends, by the way?"

Siri looked at him to see whether he was about to make fun of his spiritual connections—as he always did.

"There hasn't been a lot of activity since the floating Vietnamese last November. But then again, we haven't had too many mysteries lately."

"They only come out in times of confusion?"

"No. They're around all the time. They all make an appearance, but they don't ne-cessessarily do anything. I get an old lady sitting opposite me in the office late"—he hiccuped "excuse me, at night. She just sits there. I keep waiting for her to do something, flash me a tit or some such, but she just sits, chewing betel, staring at me."

"You know, Siri, sometimes you scare the daylights out of me." Civilai leaned over and poured the remains of the Soviet bribe into their chipped glasses. "We should finish this up before it eats through the bottom of the bottle."

"A toast to the illustrious Union of Sovalist Republicists."

"I don't think you need any more."

They quaffed the dregs and Siri got unsteadily to his feet.

"Thank God that's over. Now we can have some deluscious coffee."

The late afternoon was becoming evening.

The shadows from the instant jungle had fallen across the two pickled patriots and were climbing the concrete wall behind them. The chewy coffee was shocking them out of their Sunday stupors. Civilai made one last attempt to encourage his friend to feel at home.

"I think this place is quite charming."

"Then I'll move in with your wife and you can live here."

"Let me think about that."

"It was supposed to be a reward, but it's more like punishment, older brother. I've got busybody Miss Vong on one side of me and some corrupt local official from Oudom Xay on the other."

"Surely you could shout that a little bit louder."

Siri ignored him. "I've got a goddamned loudspeaker blaring out diatribes against the non-communist world right there at the corner of the street from five A. goddamned M. I couldn't be any more unhappy."

"All you need here is a good woman to turn it into a home. I don't suppose you've—"

"Don't."

"I was only wondering if you'd—"

"Don't."

"—contacted her. That's all."

"No. And I won't. Don't ask again."

"Seems silly to me."

Siri sulked for a moment or two. There had only been one woman, one date, since Boua had died. It was a disaster of a date. Siri knew Lah was a woman he could love. The feeling was returned. Auntie Lah had custom-made baguettes for him at her cart opposite Mahosot Hospital from the first week he arrived there. They joked, they flirted, and she made no secret of the fact she liked him.

Once Boua, his only love, his long-departed wife, had given her postmortem permission, he went at that new romance like a teenager. On the night of the fateful date when he first saw Lah waiting there, glamorous and preening like a *Likay* queen, the butterflies in his belly had almost lifted him from the seat of his motorbike.

She ran over on her unfamiliar heels and sniffed the air at his cheek. He felt the brush of her lips, and parts of him that had been in hibernation for many years began to stir. It was all marvelously portentous. He was at the precipice overlooking what he knew could be a wonderful final cycle to his life.

He was about to leap when she handed him the gift. It was beautifully wrapped and expensively heavy. She said it was something she'd found at the morning market. She said it was as if it had spoken to her. She believed it could stymie his run of bad luck. He opened the box, and all his hope caved in like some badly built temple stupa.

In the cardboard coffin lay a black amulet eroded by decades of hopeful fingers. It was attached to a fraying leather thong. Siri knew it well.

Lah smiled, expecting a smile in return from her dashing beau. But, instead, the expression on his face frightened her. His unkempt white eyebrows gathered at the center of a furrowed brow. He shook his head slowly and asked "How could you do this?"

"Wha—?"

Siri had sped off on his motorcycle clutching the amulet in his left hand, without saying another word. She watched him go with her cherry-red bottom lip hanging open. Of course she had no idea what she'd done. She thought she was showing him a kindness. She thought she was giving him a token of her affection. But it had turned out to be doom. She never saw him again and never understood why.

Siri had ridden to the Mekhong at its deepest point and hurled the amulet far out into the murky brown water. There were no coincidences any more in his life. That, he knew. Everything was inked on some sacred parchment. Malevolent spirits were in pursuit of him. The previous year at an exorcism in Khamuan, he'd been given this very amulet, an antique black stone, to ward off the evil spirits of the forest; the *Phibob*. But it had turned out to be a trick. The stone was actually a spiritual lintel that opened a gateway from their world to his. He'd been lucky to survive their attack. Now they wanted revenge on him. Lah had been selected to deliver this omen, and she was in danger as a result. It was clear that she could never be a part of his life. No matter how strongly he felt attracted to her, it was impossible.

Of course, Civilai said that was all a pile of buffalo dung. He said when the chance of a little over-seventy nooky presented itself, one shouldn't read too much into coincidence. "At our age, my little brother, these opportunities don't come along every day."

"It wasn't a coincidence. I sent those spirits packing, and in so doing I saved the soldiers that were cutting down their trees. They weren't happy about that. But I tell you, that stone had been destroyed."

"Did you see that happen with your own eyes?"

"Yes. Well, not with my own eyes. But I saw the dust before the Hmong took it out to the forest."

"Then you can't be sure it came from the stone. Mystery one solved."

"So how did it get here, to Vientiane? How did it get to the market? And of all the people who could have bought it, why Lah?"

"I'm an elder statesman with a not-inconsequential intellect. I can solve many of the conundrums that arise from the day-to-day running of a little country in the southeast of Asia. But I have a one-mystery-a-day quota," Civilai said. "Release me now. I have to get home to my dear wife. Remind me where my car is."

"You think you should drive?"

"Certainly. What is there to hit?"

Siri nodded and escorted him to the door. Civilai was right. On a Sunday afternoon in March, Vientiane had the atmosphere of a town in the talons of a deadly plague. A motorcyclist might brave the late-afternoon heat. A dog might lie on the concrete paving stones to burn off the fleas. But most folks were at home, waiting for the sun to go down.

At dusk, the girls would two-up on bicycles and ride slowly along Fangoum Road, catching some small breeze from the river and advertising their availability to boys two-upping in the opposite direction. They would still be mopping their sweating brows with their mothers' large pink handkerchiefs until long after nightfall.

Farewell the Diarrhetic

Old Auntie See lived in a shed behind a peeling white French colonial mansion that now housed five families. For a living, she bought fruit at the morning market, cut it into colorful slices, and sold it from a card table beside her back gate.

Business was never too brisk, since money for luxuries had become scarcer. As a result, her main diet was overly ripe fruit, which saw her spending much of her nights in the tin latrine behind the shed.

On that particular Sunday night, whilst engaged in her dribbly business, she thought she heard a growl. There were footsteps through the undergrowth of her uncared-for garden. They were too heavy to be those of a dog, but somehow too zigzag and rambling to be those of a person. She called out anyway: "Can't a woman have a shit in peace any more?"

There was no answer. The noises stopped. And after a few more minutes she forgot all about them. Diarrhea, in its most vindictive state, can erase even thoughts of terror.

Some twenty minutes later, she groaned and rearranged her long cotton *phasin* around her waist. She stepped through the corrugated tin door, and before she could stoop to wash her hands in the paint can basin, that thing was on her. She had no time to scream—to run—or even to turn her head to see what was biting into the back of her neck. With one swipe of its powerful arm, she was dead.

Two Dead Men on a Bicycle

Siri arrived at the hospital on Monday morning with a vodka hammer beating and a vodka sickle scything through his head. He guessed he couldn't have a worse hangover if he'd drunk the Formalin straight from the sample bottles. Every step from the motorcycle park to the morgue jarred new agony into his brain. There was no question in his mind that the Soviet Union was doomed.

He walked beneath the French MORGUE sign, carefully wiped his feet on the American WELCOME mat, and stepped inside the cool dark single-story building. He immediately sensed one or two presences, but was far too vodka'd to acknowledge them. They could wait.

He walked into his office, whose blue walls had been thoroughly whitewashed again and again until they were gray. Anything that wasn't blue suited Siri just fine. Nurse Dtui was sitting at her desk.

"Morning, Comrade Siri," she said, flashing her small, neat teeth but not stirring her large, untidy body.

"Good morning, Dtui."

Those first words of the day came out like a gravel driveway.

"Oh-ho. Have a bit of a session last night, did we?"

"A cultural experiment."

He flopped into his chair, and his head turned to percussion. He buried it in his hands.

"Looks like the experiment failed."

"No, my faithful assistant. Never assume that negative experiences teach you less than positive ones. I have it filed away that in the future, no matter how free, no matter how fascinating the squiggles on the bottle, I shall avoid Russian vodka as if it were a musthy elephant."

Dtui stood. Her uniform was bleached white and stretched across her large frame like butcher's paper around a hock of pork.

"What you need is some of my ma's herbal brew."

"Oh, no. Don't say it. Haven't I suffered enough?"

"Don't go away."

She headed for the door.

"Where's our other soldier?"

"He's in the examination room getting the new guests ready." She stopped in the doorway. "You'll like this one: two men dead on a bicycle in the middle of the street. No spare seat or luggage rack. They were going around Nam Poo fountain in the middle of town. Nothing there could have been going fast enough to hit them. They were found on top of the bike. No blood. This looks like a job for . . . dah-dah-da-dah."

"Dtui?"

". . . Super Spirit Doc."

She giggled and walked out of the office. Siri groaned. The last thing he wanted on that particular morning was to cut anyone up. He especially didn't want anything inexplicable to trouble his hurting head.

Dtui was fumbling in the back of the freezer for the corked bottle that held her mother's secret brew. Although there was a hospital ban on using the morgue freezers for personal perishables, her ma's brew looked enough like body waste to fool the most pedantic inspector. It was an evil Macbethian mix of bizarre ingredients that tasted horrible but cured just about anything.

"Wha . . . wha . . . what's that for, Dtui?" Mr. Geung was laying out the second cyclist on the spare aluminum table. Geung was a good-looking man in his forties with pronounced Down-Syndrome features and jet-black hair greased on either side of a crooked center parting. When he asked a question, he had the habit of rocking slightly where he stood. Judge Haeng at the Department of Justice, which oversaw the work of Siri and his team, was lobbying for the removal of the "moron," but Geung's condition was neither serious nor disruptive to his work. Although he often became anxious about anomalies outside the regimented pattern of his days, he was a morgue assistant par excellence. He'd been trained with infinite patience by Siri's predecessor and knew the procedures better than Dtui or Siri himself. He was strong and reliable, and he wielded a mean hacksaw.

"The boss has got himself a hangover," Dtui said.

Geung snorted a laugh. "Al . . . alcohol is the elixir of the d . . . devil."

"Was that another one of your father's wisdoms?"

"No. Comrade Dr. Siri . . . ss . . . said it when we cut open the drunk fellow on January first."

That was one other thing. You didn't want to say anything you'd live to regret when Mr. Geung was around. He didn't forget much.

The autopsy followed the standard pattern they'd settled into. Siri was beginning to sit back and let Dtui give the commentary while he took notes. She was learning the trade and hoped to be sent to the Eastern Bloc on a scholarship. Her eyes were keen, and she often noticed things that Siri had missed. The only setback to this new system was that nobody could read Siri's notes afterward. Not even Siri.

As the two bodies in the morgue hadn't been reported as missing, they would temporarily be known as Man A and Man B.

They were an ill-matched pair. Man A was neatly dressed in a white shirt. He had on an old but quite costly wristwatch, wore permanent-press slacks, and had soft, uncallused hands which suggested he wasn't used to manual labor. But, as Siri and Dtui both noticed, the most remarkable thing about him was that he was wearing socks. The March temperatures were already hitting 107 degrees. Even in those few offices where ancient French air conditioners waged battle with the heat, the best they could ever achieve was "tepid." It was *never* so cold you'd need to wear socks.

No, these socks suggested that the poor man had no choice. Since he had become coroner, Siri had been under pressure to wear the black vinyl shoes provided by the Party. It was an example of what he termed the new "shoe over substance" policy. So far, he'd been able to use his seniority and his stubborn streak to remain in his brown leather sandals. But he knew that if he were finally compressed into those toe-torturers, he certainly would have to wear socks also.

Dtui spoke his thought. "I'd say he's government."

"The socks?"

"The fingers."

She was constantly surprising him. Siri went over and held up Mr. A's hand. All the fingertips were purple: triplicate syndrome.

It was Civilai who'd coined the phrase to describe the peculiar mauve "bruising" so common in socialist bureaucracies. They were bogged down in paperwork, as there had to be copies for every department. This called into play that miracle of modern office timesaving: carbon paper.

Laos got its carbon paper, like its shoes and its hair dye, from China. So most officials that used it found more ink on themselves than on the paper. Mr. A had thumbed his share of carbon sheets.

They stripped him, bagged and labeled his clothes, and took

their allotted four color photographs of his outside. Siri noted that no shoes had arrived with the body. There was a thin trail of congealed blood at the corner of the mouth and severe bruising to the chest and abdomen.

Before beginning an internal examination, Siri decided to prepare Mr. B for the chop also. This would ultimately save time and allow them to make comparisons of their respective injuries. Siri ignored Dtui's comment that "This is how they do it at the abattoir," and asked her to voice her observations about Mr. B.

She noted that he was certainly from a different end of town than Mr. A. His clothes were threadbare and quite dirty. His hands were rough and covered in scabs of short nicks as if he'd been cut often.

"So, the question remains," Siri pondered, almost to himself, ". . . what were two men from very different backgrounds doing sharing a bicycle at two in the morning?"

"Perhaps," Dtui suggested, "this one was the chauffeur and he was taking his master home."

Geung let out one of his farmyard laughs.

"Or perhaps they weren't on the bicycle at all." Siri glared. "I'm starting to think the fact they were found with the bike was a coincidence."

"So, how did they get there?"

"Oh, I don't know everything, Miss Dtui. Perhaps the old chap ran into the government fellow when he was crossing the road."

"Yeah? And how fast would he have been pedaling to kill the pair of them?"

"Or, alternatively, the government fellow was riding a motorbike and hit the old boy."

"And . . . ?"

"And someone ran off with the motorbike."

"I suppose I could buy that one."

"Did the police bring in the bicycle, Mr. Geung?"

"It's round the b . . . round the b . . . the back."

"Good. We can take a look at it later."

They stripped Mr. B. Apart from his obviously broken neck and the massive bruising associated with vertebral artery trauma, there were no recent abrasions or visible marks on him. They finished up the film and laid him out. There the two corpses reclined on either side of the room, like temple step ornaments.

The dual autopsy took exactly two hours. Mr. A had hemorrhaging around the chest cavity and livor mortis around the main artery common in victims of high-speed collisions, so the motorcycle theory still held. Some trauma had also been sufficiently violent to rupture his testicles. From these initial examinations, Siri surmised that the broken neck had killed Mr. B, and the internal bleeding Mr. A. But there were other tests to do.

Mr. Geung cut through the tough crania with his old hacksaw, and Siri tied cotton around the brains in order to suspend them in Formalin for two or three days until they were set firm enough to cut into.

Dtui took samples of the stomach contents and blood. As they had no lab, there were only limited secrets these could disclose. The next day, Siri would take a ride over to the Lycée Vientiane, where he would coerce Teacher Oum into using the last of her science lab chemicals on color tests.

Somewhere out at the customs shed, a crate of school chemicals, kindly donated by the high-school cooperative in Vladivostok, had sat for three months collecting paperwork. Even being the national coroner didn't carry any weight in pushing that old bureaucratic bus up the hill to socialist nirvana.

Dtui, Geung, and Siri sat on their haunches around the bicycle. The rusty thing that had survived many battles would never be ridden again.

"Now, what do you suppose could cause something like this?" Siri asked of no one in particular. The frame supporting the chain was buckled and almost touching the ground. The handlebars leaned back, the seat forward.

"It looks like I sat on it," Dtui said, causing a laughing fit in Mr. Geung that took a good deal of back-slapping to arrest.

"No," Siri said at last. "It would take half a dozen Dtuis to do this. But I think I know what could. What side of the fountain were they found on?"

"Ministry side."

"I think we'd better go and take a look, don't you?"

"Is your head up to it?"

"Ah, Dtui. There's nothing like the dissection of corpses and a dollop of your ma's brew to cure a hangover."

The Ministry of Sport, Information and Culture currently and unofficially occupied a seven-story building that overlooked the non-spouting fountain at Nam Poo Square. Given the shape of things in Laos, the square was, naturally, a circle. It was surrounded by quaint and largely neglected two-storied buildings that wouldn't have felt out of place in a small southern French village. It was a sleepy square where old ladies dried white spring-roll wrappings on mesh tables and crazy Rajid the Indian walked slow laps around the dull concrete fountain.

Although the Lao weren't yet conceited enough to refer to most of their government departments as anything more grand, Vientiane people had begun to call the incongruous building that housed the sports department "The Ministry." It was probably the size of the place, rather than its grandeur, that impressed them. The old French Cultural Center had all the architectural class of a two-star hotel in a seaside resort. The Sport, Information and Culture people rattled around inside its large rooms like a destitute woman's beads in a once-full jewelry box.

Mr. Geung had stayed back at the morgue to keep an eye on the guests. Dtui, on her first investigative mission away from the hospital, stood in the middle of the road beside the angels chalked there on the asphalt. Siri was twelve meters away, with his back against the wall of The Ministry. He painted an imaginary arc with his eyebrows from the point where Dtui stood up to the top ledge of the building above him. He shook his head and walked over to the nurse.

"No good?" She asked.

"Well, it isn't impossible, but . . . I don't know. He either took one almighty running jump, or he was tossed. And if someone had thrown him, we would have found marks on his arms or legs. But we didn't."

"You don't think he might have—"

A Vespa scooter came putting around the fountain, causing Siri to leap from its path into the unsuspecting arms of Dtui.

"Dr. Siri. You romantic old thing, you."

Embarrassed, he untangled himself from her embrace. The scooter stopped a few meters further on, and the rider, a trim attractive man in his forties, looked back and laughed. Inspector Phosy got down, hoisted the silly vehicle onto its stand, and hurried back with a handshake at the ready. Siri grabbed the hand, and the two men patted each other's backs as they embraced.

"Hot, isn't it?"

"Damned hot."

"How's my favorite policeman?"

"Dr. Siri. I thought you were dead."

"Don't you be so sure I'm not." They broke apart, and Siri looked along the street. "That's a very impressive cop bike you have. Lilac's the crime-suppression color of the year, I hear."

"Be kind, comrade. These are hard times. We have to take what we can get." He looked over Siri's shoulder. "Good health, Dtui. You haven't lost any weight."

"And you're no better looking."

She shook his hand warmly.

"So," Siri asked. "How did you get this case?"

"They put me on anything with the word 'government' attached to it. As soon as Dtui called and suggested the victim could be a government official, they took me out of the cupboard. How hard do you think this is going to be? Was it a suicide?"

"I don't know. It's odd. Unless he was trying to fly, I don't see why he wouldn't just drop from the roof. He'd be just as dead without trying to reach the fountain."

"All right, then. Let's see if we can get any information from the information department."

They walked together through the elegant wooden doors and found themselves in a foyer containing nothing but a table. On the table was a small, hand-written sign that said ALL INQUIRIES UPSTAIRS.

Their footsteps echoed up the teak staircase. They noted how stuffy the place felt. Despite the heat, most of the windows hadn't been opened since the Americans left. (French culture had briefly been supplanted there by American language classes before the building's current manifestation.) The only culture not in evidence was Lao. Or perhaps it was.

On the second floor, they passed two rooms empty of furniture and life. The third door was slightly ajar, and through the gap they could see two metal cabinets, an uneven shelf with all its books resting at the low end, and a desk with a man on it.

He slept in his undershirt with a blissful expression on his young face. His ironed white shirt made a scarecrow over his chair. Although it was twenty minutes past one, and officially office hours, Phosy knocked politely and said "I'm sorry."

As the man didn't stir, he was about to knock a second time when Siri pushed past him into the room. The doctor was a remarkably patient man, but he had no time for incompetence in the government sector. He and Boua had fought for most of their lives to end corrupt systems and he had no intention of being part of one. In his most officious voice, he belted out: "Good God, man! What do you think you're doing? This is a government department, not a rest home. What if there was some sporting emergency or something?"

Phosy and Dtui raised their eyebrows at each other.

The man came out of his dream flailing, sending a stand of nicely sharpened pencils on a flight across the room. He leaped from the desktop and into his shoes. The visitors watched as he ran around the desk, gathered his shirt, and put it on. He was a plain-looking man with a naturally confused expression. He sat on the chair, fastened his shirt buttons, and, as if they hadn't witnessed the entire resurrection, asked his visitors, "May I help you?"

Phosy, smiling, handed him a mimeographed sheet with his photograph stapled to a top corner. This was his ID. The man scrutinized it with great care.

"Police?" he concluded.

"Very good. There was a death in front of The Ministry last night. Maybe early this morning. Are you missing anyone?"

"Now, that's hard to say."

"Why?"

"We're missing people all the time. Staff off in other provinces. People off sick. We haven't seen the head or deputy head for over a week."

"Isn't there some schedule? Some way to check who is supposed to be where?"

"Hmm. No."

"Where's the office that arranges all the trips?"

"Oh, right. That would be me."

"And you don't keep some kind of list?"

"It's a good idea, but nobody's ever asked before. You'd have to go from room to room and see who's missing."

So that's what they did. Siri was impressed that the department of information could provide so little of it. The search began on the second floor and worked its way up. The young man took them to rooms and introduced them to barely-stressed secretaries and average men whose jobs appeared to be to read newspapers, magazines, and novels.

Siri described the dead man at each office in turn, but soon realized that he could be talking about half the men who worked there. They all wore stay-press trousers and vinyl shoes, and were at varying stages of triplicate syndrome.

The administration rooms on the fifth floor were mostly empty, and the door leading to the top two floors was apparently locked. While the staff ran around looking for a key to open it, ever-resourceful Dtui noticed that there was already a key in the lock from the other side. They knocked and shouted for someone to come down and let them up, but when their banging was met by stony silence the worst was assumed.

"Who works up there?" Siri asked.

"Archives," said the young man. "It's like our history department. You know? Preservation and the like."

Siri wondered to himself how much priority the regime was placing on safeguarding the country's heritage, given that there weren't even funds available to station guards at the cultural sites. Anyone who fancied a coffee-table bust of the Buddha could just go and help himself.

After no more than two minutes on her knees, with the deft use of her watch pin and the careful placement of a newspaper beneath the door, Dtui was able to remove and retrieve the key on the other side of the door. Phosy looked on in admiration.

"You know? There are one or two unsolved burglary cases from the old regime. . . ."

"Couldn't have been me, Officer. I wore gloves. Oops."

They reinserted the key and opened the door, and Phosy led the way up the staircase to the sixth and seventh floors, which were little more than a few rooms attached to the roof.

Siri sensed some unsettled force as he followed the others. He didn't feel confident enough of his instincts to warn anyone to be careful.

The main archive department was one large room on the seventh floor. It was in a terrible state. Pots were shattered and spread across the floor. Maps and stone rubbing sheets had been ripped from the walls. Beyond the mess, two things caught Phosy's eye. The large glass French windows were open, the glass smashed and the catch broken. Beyond them was a trajectory that would have taken a potential jumper swiftly to the chalk angel marks on the road beside the fountain. But he'd have had to take a run at it.

He also took note of the parallel shoes on the floor beside the overturned desk. With all the broken crockery around, it was unlikely the man would have taken them off before the jump. So the chaos had apparently not yet occurred. Phosy stuck his head out the window and looked either side. There was no way an assailant could have left the room via the window and escaped without a parachute. He turned back to see the others starting to clean up the mess.

"All right. Nobody touches anything till my people have had a chance to look around. Now, Mr. . . . what's your name?"

"Santhi."

"Mr. Santhi. Who works in this office?"

"Mrs. Bounhieng. She's off having another baby. And Mr. Chansri. He's the director of the archives. And Mr. Khampet."

"And do either of those two gentlemen fit the description of the chap in the morgue?"

"Oh. Mr. Khampet. Definitely. Mr. Chansri's an older gentleman, and a little overweight."

"And where might we find the director of the archives?" Santhi shifted uneasily and looked at the ground. "Did you hear the question?"

"Yes."

"Well?"

"He could be at Tong Kankum market."

"I take it he isn't on ministry business."

"He sells fish."

"Right."

"I probably shouldn't have told you. But you understand. We don't get paid a lot here, so some of us supplement. . . ."

"Mr. Santhi. I'm not a government inspector." Phosy looked across to see Siri on his haunches looking beneath the heavy wooden workbench. "What's that?"

"You see this?"

The detective walked across and looked under the bench.

"An old chest."

"No. It's a lot more than an old chest. Look. It has the royal seal."

Embossed onto a solid teak box, an improbable three-headed elephant stood on a podium like some circus freak at the That Luang Festival. It sheltered beneath a multi-tiered umbrella. Only time had removed its glitter. Siri lowered his voice. "The chest has a lot of energy, too. Whatever's in there is giving off a lot of aggression."

"Siri, you aren't having one of your supernatural moments?"

Very few people knew of the extent of Siri's mystic connections. In fact, only Civilai, Dtui, and Geung, in his own way, knew just how weird the doctor was. Siri had only recently become aware of his gifts himself. On the same visit to his birthplace in Khamuan when the *Phibob* had been roused, he'd been informed of something remarkable. In truth, he still didn't believe all the things he'd heard. According to the elders of one small village, Siri was the re-embodiment of Yeh Ming, a powerful Hmong shaman who had lived over a thousand years ago. Since the discovery, Siri had become aware of amazing powers that lurked somewhere deep inside him. As yet, he was unsure of how to use them, and in many ways they frightened the daylights out of him. He'd never directly informed Phosy of his unbidden gifts, but the policeman's instincts told him all he needed to know.

Siri reached out his hand toward the chest, and then withdrew it suddenly as if a shock had warned him off.

"I'd tell your people to be very careful of this, if I were you. Very careful."

Siri's dream that night didn't answer any questions for him. Mr. A, now positively identified as Khampet, was floating slowly down through the air toward Nam Poo fountain. He floated like a hawk but had a look of horror on his face. The ends of long staves of wood were nailed to his hands and feet. Another entered the back of his neck and appeared to go up into his head. But these didn't seem to worry him. He was more concerned about what was behind him, and whatever that was, it didn't appear in the dream shot. The occult cameraman wasn't giving anything away.

But just for a brief second, not long enough to be certain, Siri may have seen a line of witnesses on the roof above. They seemed happy—or perhaps *satisfied* would be a better description. In that brief second, he had a feeling they were old performers, the type that wore thick makeup and traditional Lao costumes. They may also have been applauding, but it's possible that Siri had been trying so hard to see something, he'd imagined the whole thing.

That's what he believed when he awoke. As was common after he'd had one of his dreams, he found himself in a state that may have been consciousness, or may have been a continuation of the dream. These were the scary moments when the visitors felt so real they could have been in the room with him.

It was quiet. The stars were still blurred by the heat rising from the hot earth, so he was certain he hadn't been asleep long. He was on the veranda behind his mausoleum. The mosquito net shimmied from a rare puff of summer breeze. It moved again. And again. It was swaying gently in time to some slow but regular stimulus.

Siri turned his head and looked into the darkness, and into the dull eyes of a bear. It was so close, its breath moved the net. It was close enough that Siri could see fresh blood at the corner of its mouth; close enough for him to smell the decay on its teeth.

It was sitting, watching the doctor. He felt its power over him. But Siri wasn't fearful. Yes, he believed this was unreal in some way, but he also had an instinct that the animal wasn't there to hurt him. The creature, its inspection over, rose painfully, turned, and walked off into the mobile jungle.

When Siri next awoke, it was certainly morning and the sun was threatening to rise over Miss Vong's well-scrubbed house. Before he could forget it, and before the government loudspeakers could begin their obnoxious prattle, he reached for the notebook on the table beside the cot. He lit the cooking-oil lamp and wrote down his dream.

Saloop dragged himself toward the light like some obese moth and put his head on the cot. Siri scratched it.

"You didn't happen to see a bear in the yard this morning, did you?" Siri asked.

As always, Saloop kept his secrets to himself. He'd neglected his duties. He'd been off romancing the bitch at the ice-works. He smelled the intruder when he got back, sure enough. It wasn't a scent he'd come across before. But it was something big and terrifying.

A Day at the Maul

Mr. Geung was sweeping the deceased cockroaches from the morgue when Siri arrived the next morning.

"Morning, Mr. Geung."

"G . . . good health, comrade doctor."

"Any new guests today?"

He was expecting a "no" in response. Geung laughed and looked to the sky as if Siri's consistent question were the most wondrous greeting a man could receive. He never tired of it. Siri often considered climbing inside his friend's mind to enjoy some of his simple pleasures.

"New guest in r . . . r . . . room one, comrade doctor."

"Oh, no." Siri moaned. "Isn't it getting a bit crowded in room one?"

There was only the one freezer. The last Siri had known, Mr. A and Mr. B were already bunked in there on makeshift bamboo rafts that doubled the occupancy potential.

Geung snorted a laugh. "N . . . n . . . no. Mr. A and Mr. B went home already."

"Somebody came for them?"

"Yes."

Siri walked into the office to find Dtui at her desk poring over the pictures in one of Siri's old French pathology textbooks. As she studied the black-and-white photo of a man who'd been sliced in half by a locomotive, she chewed on a rice snack wrapped in pig intestine.

"Do you recall the good old days when I'd come in here and find you reading Thai comics?" Siri asked.

"Good health, Doctor."

"Good health. I hear A and B have left us."

Dtui put down her greasy snack, wiped her hands on a surgical mask, and picked up the police report.

"Mr. B. Now Kampong Siriwongsri. Glass factory laborer by day. Second-shift security guard by night. He was on his way to work. His wife identified the body and they took him to the temple to get him ready. Mr. A apparently didn't have anyone to love him, and don't *we* know what that feels like. So the Ministry of Sport, Information and Culture has taken responsibility and arranged a cheap ceremony at Ong Deu temple."

Siri's mind suddenly jumped to his own death. Who'd take responsibility when he huffed his last breath? Who'd pay for his funeral at some nondescript temple? His friends were all broke. Would Judge Haeng discover some unmined vein of generosity and arrange for the Department of Justice to give him a state funeral? Some hope.

"So . . ." Dtui was still answering ". . . it all fits. Mr. B is riding to his second job when Mr. A drops out of the sky and lands on top of him: chances—eleven million to one against. A breaks B's neck, buckles the bike, and kills himself. Case closed."

"Except. . . ."

"Except for why. But that's the police's problem, not ours, right?"

"Aren't you just a little curious, Dtui?"

"I'm peeing myself with anticipation."

"Well," he blushed. "That's good. I mean, curiosity's good in this job. Keep it up."

*   *   *

The poor lady in the freezer had obviously been mauled. The wounds were over twenty-four hours old, and the insects and even her own cat had started on her before she went off from the heat. Her clothes were shredded and black with blood, while her skin was blanched white. There were bite marks on her body, the most traumatic of these being at her neck. Those areas of skin that hadn't been bitten were raked with scratch marks.

"They found her in the bushes beside her shanty." Dtui was behind the doctor as he stood at the open freezer, looking at the mess that Auntie See had become.

"Didn't anyone report it when it happened? There must have been a hell of a lot of noise."

"Nope."

"What's happening to people? Didn't we used to care for our neighbors?"

"Perhaps they thought it was just a dog fight."

But there was something wrong with that premise. Even before an autopsy, just looking into the dark freezer, he knew it wasn't possible. From the size of the visible wounds, the separation between the individual claws, he had a strong feeling this was no dog attack.

The autopsy was new to all of them. Siri was in no position to read up on the latest forensic pathology techniques from around the globe. For one thing, they didn't get a lot of useful information from the outside world. For another, all the advances were being made in the United States, and Siri's English stank. He was fluent in Thai, French, and Vietnamese, but these had apparently filled up his language tank, and all attempts at adding English overflowed hopelessly.

But if the rest of the world ever learned Lao, he would certainly have become an authority on innovation in a morgue.

Here he was with a body covered in bite marks, and he needed to confirm whether they were from dogs. So with a modicum of genius, he sent Geung off to the kitchen with a requisition form and started to create dams with adhesive bandages around the most profound marks. When Geung got back, Dtui mixed a thick solution of agar, and they poured it into pools on Auntie See.

"Is this standard procedure?" Dtui wanted to know.

"Well, I hear they use plaster of paris in the West, but we can't afford that. They don't even have any in the 'breaks and fractures' department of the hospital. So we'll have to see how this works. Just don't get peckish and raid the freezer before they set."

"I won't."

After a few hours, the agar was solid and looking pretty as birthday-party treats with little turrets of teeth prints. Geung moved them to the refrigerator, and they took Auntie See out for an internal examination.

As a New Year's present, the Justice Department had furnished the morgue with a Soviet air conditioner so the men no longer had to work in shorts and undershirts. Dtui no longer had to stand in front of the open freezer door to cool off. But the stifling temperature outside that day had defeated USSR technology. There was probably a higher setting, but Siri couldn't read Russian. So as they stooped over Auntie See, Mr. Geung had to constantly mop brows with a towel.

All they learned was that the lady had lost a great deal of blood. The attack was the probable cause of death, as she had certainly been alive when it began. Her bowels were a mess, but there was nothing life-threatening there. She was otherwise in good shape and should have been able to fight off any normal suburban predator.

Everything came down to the size of the wounds. That's what continued to worry Siri. While Dtui typed up the report and

Geung scrubbed down the examination room, he studied the marks on the agar molds. He used a ruler to measure the size of the jaw and the spread of the claw marks.

By 11:30, when his assistants were in the dissection room labeling jars, Siri, for no other reason than the dream of the previous morning, had come to the illogical conclusion that Auntie See had been attacked and killed by a bear.

It was lunchtime. Civilai had carried his rolls down to the river-bank and was sitting on the log, waiting for his lunch partner to arrive. He was moderately engrossed in the *Siang Pasason* news-paper when Siri tapped him on the shoulder.

"Excuse me, sir. Do you mind if I join you?"

"Well, all right. Until someone better comes along."

"Like Crazy Rajid?"

"He'd do. But see. He spends most of his days on his knees in the water."

They looked out to the narrow band of river that remained at the end of the dry season. Rajid's bald head poked from the water like a happy black penis. He was the town nutcase. Nobody knew which traveling Indian family had deserted him as a child some fifteen years before. He was just discovered one day sitting on the steps of the Black Stupa. Locals fed him regularly without question, and he repaid them by smiling and spreading his immutable happiness around Vientiane. He had no home and no need of one.

"In this heat, I envy the fellow."

"It is hot, isn't it?"

"Damned hot."

Siri sat and started to unwrap his baguette. Since their abortive date, Mrs. Lah had shifted her franchise from the hos-pital. His lunch now came from a Vietnamese woman at the end of his lane. She offered two choices: sweet or savory. He could never guess what was inside, just by looking. He was often none the wiser after the contents reached his palette. Still, food was fuel.

"Anything interesting in the paper?"

Civilai laughed. Printed news under a one-party system rarely exposed, unearthed, or titillated.

"Czech skiing conditions are improving."

"That's a relief."

"Football results from Albania. Part seventeen of Lenin's life story. Our military attaché's in Cuba."

"Anything about Laos?"

"Laos? Now you're asking. Laos. Laos. Wait. Here. A photo of happy smiling farm workers in Savanaketh above a story of a bumper cabbage harvest."

"They're standing in a rice field."

"Maybe they're taking a break."

Civilai scrunched up the newspaper and threw it over his shoulder. He was a brilliant man who tired easily of bull. He despaired of Laos's potential that was being wasted by his plodding colleagues. But he definitely agreed that it was far better to be a plodding communist than a rampant capitalist.

He looked across the Mekhong toward the Thai fascists and bit into his homemade roll. In this heat, he lacked the enthusiasm to eat. There was so little meat on his bones, he was afraid that if he didn't stop sweating soon, there wouldn't be anything left of him. He smiled as he remembered his morning meeting.

"Have you heard about the senator's visit?"

"The only way I hear anything is through you, comrade."

"Well, we've had a delegation from Washington."

"They want their bombs back?"

"They're insisting that we give them access to look for MIA's."

"What's an MIA?"

"It's a military person who gets lost in battle."

"Wait. I thought they claimed they didn't have any combat troops in Laos."

"That's right."

"So how did any soldiers get lost here?"

"Perhaps they had their maps upside down."

"And do we actually have lost Americans here?"

"I haven't seen any. But you can never tell what the LPLA will get up to. The Yanks say they've got evidence that there are MIA's held in camps up on the border."

"And they're insisting . . ."

"Yes. There's a lot of political pressure over there to bring their heroes back home."

"Well, if they insist, I suppose we'll have to cooperate."

"That's right. Wouldn't want them to start a war or anything."

"What do we get out of it?"

"Aid."

"They've offered us aid?"

"Yes."

"See? I told you they'd have guilty consciences."

By the time they'd plowed their way through the sandwiches and were enjoying some fruit, both men were in their undershirts and seriously thinking about joining Rajid in the murky water.

"Any interesting dead people this week?"

"Well, I'm sure you heard about the chap from Info and Culture."

"I read the first installment of the report. Can't see any reason for the fellow killing himself, though."

"I think something happened up there that drove him to it. It's the archive department. Do you know of anything official concerning the Royal Family?"

"You mean, apart from stripping them of their titles, humiliating them in public, kicking them out of the palace, and stealing their money?"

"Yeah, apart from that. Something concerning the DSIC."

"Why do you ask?"

"There was a trunk up there with a royal seal. It was angry."

"An angry seal?"

"No, the trunk was angry. I don't know what was in it, but I felt an incredible force."

"Enough to throw a man off a roof?"

"Could be."

It was two that afternoon when a second man found himself in a hurry to get away from the Ministry of Sport, Information and Culture. Despite falling four flights of stairs and landing on his head, Constable Nui somehow managed to cheat death. Much of him was broken, and there was some serious internal bleeding that needed emergency surgery to stem. But by five, it looked like he might make it through the night.

Siri and Inspector Phosy stood at the end of the bed watching the constable's wife and sisters setting up camp around him. With so few nurses available, families were encouraged to stay the night and look after their own. If they brought bedding, food, and any medicines they could lay their hands on, all the better.

"We won't be able to talk to him tonight," Phosy whispered.

"What was he doing up there?" Siri asked.

Phosy led the doctor outside into the hall. "We'd just finished checking out the office. The only thing left was that box of yours. There wasn't a keyhole or a catch or anything like that. There didn't seem any way of opening it. So we sent Constable Nui off to get a crowbar."

"Risky."

"What would you have done?"

"Left it well alone."

"Well, we couldn't do that. This is a possible murder inquiry. Anyway, as we were on our way out, Nui passed us on his way in. I told him to open the chest and bring whatever was inside to the station. Next thing I hear, he's face down on the fifth-floor landing."

"Did he get the chest open?"

"No. There are splinters where he tried to force in the metal bar, but he didn't make any impression on the lid. The trouble is, now none of our men are prepared to go anywhere near it. They say it's jinxed. So it looks like I'll have to do it myself."

"Phosy, can I ask you to leave it alone for a while? You'll have to trust me about this. Give me some time to find out what's in there, will you? Please?"

"I shouldn't."

"It's really important."

Phosy thought about it. "I'll give you three days. I can't bluff beyond that. I'll tell the boss it's a national treasure and we have to wait for the key."

"Thanks."

They walked out of the stuffy hospital building and into an early evening sunshine that still dazzled and blasted them. They stood in the shade of a large henna tree, but there was no breeze to cool them down.

"Hot, isn't it?"

"Damned hot."

"Phosy, can I ask you a silly question?"

"Sure."

"Have there been any reports of . . . any sightings of . . . well, wild animals around town?"

He assumed Phosy would laugh, but instead he answered very matter-of-factly.

"Only the bear."

Siri looked at him, astonished.

"There's a bear loose?"

"That ragged old heap they kept at the back of the Lan Xang. It got out somehow a few days ago. I'm surprised it had the legs to make it to the wall, let alone over it. Someone reported they'd seen it up by the memorial. God knows how it got up there. There are a couple of army people out with a net looking for it."

He noticed Siri's troubled expression. "You got a reason for asking?"

"I think you'd better come to the morgue and take a look at something."

Siri rode his old motorbike slowly along Lan Xang Avenue on his way home that evening. Families sat by the roadside hoping to catch some breeze from passing cars, waiting for the night to bring relief from the stifling day. Siri was so deep in thought, he'd forgotten to turn on his lights. When suddenly the shadow of the Anusawari monument loomed up in front of him, he flicked the switch and drilled a little hole of light into its base.

On the strength of what he'd seen in the morgue, Phosy had phoned police headquarters and suggested they get an armed unit on the streets looking for the bear. There was now a shoot-to-kill order out on it.

Two things troubled Siri. First was the gap in his knowledge of wild animals. In all his years of jungle campaigns, he'd never seen a live bear. He'd seen several dead, with bullet holes, tied to wooden staves. He'd eaten their meat. But none of that really educated him about the lifestyle of the animal.

He'd read stories of North American grizzlies and polar bears ripping people to shreds. Yet in all his years, he hadn't once heard of an Asian black bear attack. Perhaps the victims didn't live to tell the tale. Then again, with all the maltreatment this old girl had suffered over the years, she could have been out for revenge.

After work, he'd stopped at the Lan Xang and seen the state of the cage she'd been kept in. He talked to one of the long-term chambermaids, who told him how cruel people could be to her. He needed to find an animal expert. He wanted to know just what this sad creature was capable of.

He rode through the permanently open gates into the huge flat concrete yard that five months earlier had been the site of the That Luang Festival. Thousands of people had jostled and laughed and flirted there. Now it was like some large school playground during exams.

He pulled up beside the lonely white memorial dedicated to the Unknown Soldier. At the far end of the ground, the custard-yellow stupa of That Luang, in need of some attention, stared back. Some hundred meters away, a little boy in underpants kicked a tin can. Its noise echoed loudly back and forth between the two monuments.

Here was where they had sighted the bear. That was Monday, just before midnight. He looked across the yard, beyond the stupa to the road. And on the far side of that road was his own lane.

This was the second thing that worried him. The bear had come to him in his sleep early that morning. But if the bear had actually materialized as a spirit, it had to be dead. That was logical. So why had nobody found its body? And if it wasn't dead, that meant the foul-breathed creature that woke him had been alive and still dripping with the blood of its victim.

He turned off his engine twenty meters from his house and wheeled the bike into his front yard, but Miss Vong still caught him. She had to shout to be heard above the loudspeaker booming from the corner of the street. It was detailing how long to soak jackfruit skins to make the best hair conditioner.

"Good evening, comrade doctor. Hot, isn't it? I've just made some nice taro gruel."

"Good for you, Miss Vong."

"I'll bring you some over."

"No, thank you."

"Yes, I will. You have a shower and I'll be there in half an hour."

He was about to make an excuse but her head was already back inside her gate. She was a thoroughly annoying woman, spindly and plain as a hand-rolled cigarette. She'd been his neighbor in town before the apartment house they had lived in blew up, and the planning department assumed they'd want to be close in their new allocation. Thankfully, her work at the Education Department kept her out of Siri's hair for long periods.

He stood in front of his own gate and looked at the larger, far more beautiful house of his other neighbor, who was a government cadre from Oudom Xay. The man's silent children were riding in the street on their brand-new bicycles. Scotch whiskey cartons and a stereo packing case had been stacked beside the dustbins for a month so everyone could see just how proudly corrupt the man was.

Siri wondered what huge favor was being repaid to this small-town headman from the north who sat on a rocking chair on his porch every evening cleaning a pistol. He ignored all his neighbors, just as he seemed to take no interest in his own family. If he worked, he did so in the hours when Siri was sleeping.

Saloop barked a welcome from forty meters down the lane and plodded happily toward home. Siri watched his belly swing from side to side and wondered where he was getting fed. The bucket of rice and scraps Siri left out in the morning was invariably untouched by evening.

"Welcome home, brave housedog."

Saloop stretched up for a headrub.

"You realize the house could have been broken into while you were off doing whatever it is you do?"

In fact, that wasn't true. No breaking would have been necessary. With all known criminals under lock and key on the islands in Nam Ngum Reservoir, few people bothered to lock their doors now. To be honest, Siri didn't have anything worth stealing anyway.

He removed a mysterious object from his motorbike and carried it into the house. It was wrapped and taped in a blanket. Saloop followed curiously, wagging his tail. The doctor lit a lamp and took his secret all the way through to his yard to a grave he'd pre-dug for it. He'd estimated the length almost perfectly. In that far corner of the garden, in a spot hidden from prying eyes, he buried the blanket and what it contained.

He was brushing the earth from his trousers when he noticed the corrugated fence. It separated his home from one that was under construction at the back. Eventually they'd get around to building a wall. When the workers had put up this fence, it had been nailed firmly to four bamboo posts that marked the edge of his plot. It was eight feet tall and had probably been a temporary border to many homes before this.

But it was no longer fixed. At his end, it hung from one single tack and was slightly buckled, as if someone had leaned heavily against it and popped out the nails.

He lifted the flap, held up his lamp, and looked at the slow progress of the foundations there. He saw the piles of sand, still where they'd been when he moved in. But there was something curious about the nearest pile. He went through the gap and knelt down to get a better look.

There were footprints—two clear ones—which were neither human nor dog. Both were pointing in his direction. A shudder crept up his spine. Could it really have been the killer bear in the living flesh that had woken him that morning?

If so, why was Siri still alive?

Das Capital Royal

"Civilai? It's Siri."

"Siri? You're using a telephone. Next thing they know, you'll be—"

"Right. But no time for sarcasm just now."

"Oh? Okay. What do you want?"

"I need an animal expert."

"Any particular breed?"

"Bears."

"You never fail to astound me, Dr. S. I'll ask around."

"Thank you."

"Oh. And I think I've got something on your mysterious chest at the DSIC."

"Excellent. You can tell me all about it at lunch."

Siri put down the receiver, thanked the hospital clerk, and walked back to the morgue. But even though there was a lot to be learned from Civilai that day, Siri wasn't going to be able to make lunch. In fact, although he didn't know it yet, he wasn't even going to be in Vientiane.

The sand had been packed quite tightly at the construction site, but the cement Siri mixed the night before had still spread a good deal. He and Dtui sat at his desk comparing the concrete cast with the agar scratch marks. They measured the separation between the claws. It wasn't identical but the difference wasn't great enough to preclude them coming from the same creature.

"Dtui, if it was the bear that ripped auntie See apart, that same bear came to visit me on Tuesday."

"Wow. You saw it?"

"I thought it was a dream. But dreams don't pull down fences and leave footprints."

"How come you're still alive?"

"That's a good question."

"And one you'll have to wait for an answer to."

Siri and Dtui both looked up to see where the whiny voice had come from. In the doorway, a thin, well-dressed man in his early thirties stood with his hands on his hips. The hot weather had inflamed his acne to the point that it seemed to glow on his cheeks.

"Goodness, Judge Haeng. What an honor." Siri smiled.

Dtui made the man a polite *nop* with her palms tightly together. "Good health, Comrade Judge."

The man responded to neither the *nop* nor the words. He sat at Dtui's desk and fanned himself in exaggerated fashion with the papers he carried.

"Hot, isn't it?" she tried again, but he ignored her.

"If I could trust any of the fools in my office not to run off and go shopping before they brought you a message, I wouldn't have to be here myself. But this is an emergency, and it has been entrusted to me."

Mr. Geung had seen the judge arrive and had gone for a glass of cool ice water from the canteen. It was one of the services he happily provided. When he got back, he put it down in front of the ruddy man and looked at his blemished skin as he said "Good h . . . h . . . health, Com . . . Comr . . ."

"Heaven help us. Does he ever get to the end of a sentence?"

"He's overwhelmed by your omnipotence." Siri smiled again.

"I'm not about to consume any liquids in this place, am I? Tell him to take this away."

"He speaks Lao quite well."

"I'm sure he does, eventually. Take it away." He despaired of the fact that Geung ignored him and stood his ground, just as he despaired because his department was hiring a mongoloid when they had the budget for a "normal" person. But Siri was unshakable. He said the day Geung left, he'd follow.

"What's so urgent?"

"It's a delicate matter. You two go and find something to do."

Siri smiled at Dtui. "I think he means you two."

She stood very slowly, walked across the room, took Geung's hand in an extravagant manner, and led him to the door. "Come, Mr. Geung. Let's go and get started on those excreta samples before they go lumpy."

She looked back and caught Haeng squirming. When they'd gone, the judge leaned forward and said "Siri, there's a military helicopter waiting for you at Wattay."

"Why?"

Before answering, Haeng took a deep breath. He'd run head-first into Siri's stubborn streak on a few occasions. "You're going to Luang Prabang."

Siri seemed to consider this for a moment. "When?"

"Right now. My car's outside."

"But—"

"This is a national security matter. It's top secret. That's why I didn't risk using the telephone."

"What's it all about?"

"I'm not terribly clear myself."

"Then you needn't have worried about the phone."

"Siri, this order comes from the very top. I don't have time for any of your temperamental rantings. There's no choice."

Siri wasn't in the least threatened by the young judge or impressed by orders from the "very top." But he could see that Haeng was. For the sake of future cooperation from the Justice Department, he decided not to give the man a hard time. And there was one other, more personal, reason why a free trip to Luang Prabang wouldn't be such a bad thing.

Luang Prabang was the Royal Capital, the birthplace of his wife, and a very scenic spot, so he'd heard. It was the historic seat of the Lan Xang empire: *Lan*, a million, *Xang*, elephants. It was in the mountains and some fifteen degrees cooler than the steampot he was in now. A night up north might not be half-bad at that. He spoke with an excitement in his voice that surprised the judge.

"Well, let's not keep the army helicopter waiting."

"Eh? Do you need—I don't know, a toothbrush or anything?"

Following a similar urgent summons south the previous year, Siri had kept a permanently packed overnight bag in the office. Personally, he traveled light. Most of it was morgue equipment, gloves and wraps.

"No. Give me five minutes with my team, and I'll join you in the car."

To Haeng, this was a victory of sorts. His first. He decided it deserved a victory lap. He let loose with one of his renowned maxims.

"That's the spirit, Siri. It's moments like this that make the socialist system so great. When the call to arms comes the committed cadre, even on his honeymoon, would gladly climb off his young wife at the crucial moment sooner than let down the Party."

If that were so, Siri thought to himself, it might explain the frustrated look he'd often seen on the faces of so many Party members.

The old Mi-8 "Hip" helicopter swung back and forth beneath its rotor like a poor baby's crib. The young Lao pilots were friendly enough, but they seemed petrified to find themselves in control of the beast. Siri assumed that they hadn't long ago passed through the Soviet training course that had farmboys still warm from the backs of buffalo inside a cockpit in three months.

After the initial "Hot isn't it?" "Damned hot," there was too much noise for a conversation. So Siri spent the ninety-minute flight in thought. He was on his way to a place that symbolized Laos to the few people in the outside world who had a clue where Laos was. Yet to him it was another era, another country altogether.

He had been born somewhere around 2446: the year the West knew as 1903. There was only one person who could have confirmed that, and she'd kept it to herself. So when it eventually came to filling out forms, Siri settled on a date that more or less matched his body.

He was born into a chaotic Laos that existed because the French colonists said it did. They'd drawn lines here and there on maps, and all that fell within them was known as the administrative district of Laos, the fifth piece in France's Indo-China set. It seemed not to matter a bit that some thirty ethnic groups gathered in that bureaucratic net were neither of Lao origin, nor subservient to the French. When you trawl for featherback, picking up the odd buk fish is unavoidable.

Despite this nicely inked border, Laos was a divided country. The king, with French permission, ruled the areas in the north around Luang Prabang. The floating southern provinces, once a separate kingdom, had changed hands ten years earlier from the Thais to the French. They were underpopulated and underproductive and left the invaders with more headaches than looted profits. But as the French still had fertile Thai territory in their sights, the south of Laos was a necessary stepping stone. It was into this area of administrative annoyance that Siri had arrived in the world.

The first eight years of his life were a blank and a mystery. His early recollections were of an aunt: a stiff-backed, broad-nosed woman who told him nothing of his parents. And he knew nothing about her. She'd been a rare educated woman, and, between tending her rice and her livestock, she schooled the boy in her rattan hut.

She was a humorless hag with as much love in her as a dag on a goat's backside. But Siri had a huge appetite for learning. He'd wondered since whether he'd tried so hard to study because he wanted the woman's respect. If she did respect his hard work, she never let him know.

His home then had been Khamuan, a lush forested province that leaned against the mountains of the Annamite Highlands. But when he was ten years old, the woman set off with him on an unannounced two-day trek. It took them to a paved road, a sight he'd never before seen. There were to be many more spectacles. A truck took them along that marvelously potholed road all the way to a city. It was called Savanaketh, and it stood on the east bank of the Mekhong.

The woman must have told him a dozen times to close his mouth as she dragged him around that city; but to a boy from the bush, it was a wonder. She found a temple she'd been searching for, and he sat on a wall in front of it while she talked to the abbot in the refectory. As she walked past Siri on her way out, she muttered something about being good, and that was the last he ever saw of her.

The boy, who knew nothing of Buddhism, was shorn, draped in itchy saffron robes, and turned into a novice. He studied the scriptures until they oozed from his ears like sap from a bloated rubber tree, but he also discovered another world of knowledge. There was very little written in the Lao language in those days, a situation that hadn't improved much since. To really become a scholar, he had to fathom the mystery of the shelves of thick books that filled a small room behind the abbey. They were all written in French.

Madame Le Saux was a missionary with the tiny Église St. Étoine, who had come to Laos for the very purpose of rescuing third-world children from poverty and ignorance. Like a large number of upper-class French spinsters, she didn't possess many skills that poor, ignorant Lao children would find useful. So, in Siri, she suddenly had her raison d'être. He was her boy, her apprentice, her justification for being there.

She had the ego to believe that Siri's rapid grasp of French was of her doing. He took to the language like a lizard to a fluorescent lamp, and by the end of two years had consumed most of the books in the temple library. She gave him the tools, but the labor was his alone.

He scored top marks on the entrance test for the exclusive lycée, and his mentor gladly paid all the fees. By the time he was eighteen, he'd absorbed everything the school had to offer and was still hungry for more. Strings were pulled, documents of noble birth were forged, and Siri had a scholarship to a reasonable medical school in Paris. There he met, wooed, and wed Boua.

In 1939, with Hitler already making reservations for the trip to Paris, Siri and Boua boarded an airplane belonging to the fledgling Air France Company that took them to Bangkok. He held his new medical certificate. She held a nursing diploma and a letter of introduction from the French Communist Party to one of its founder members: Ho Chi Minh.

So, there it was in a nutshell. Poverty led him to religion, religion to education, education to lust, lust to communism. And communism had brought him back full circle to poverty. There was a Ph.D. dissertation waiting to be written about such a cycle.

Through the scratched window, he saw the sun reflect golden from half a dozen temple stupas. Two rivers converged, and a white shrine, like a delicious meringue, sat on top of a hill overlooking the old royal palace. This had to be Luang Prabang.

Carbon Corpses

In a small dark room behind the Luang Prabang district office, something was wrapped up in an old U.S. Army parachute. The unfriendly local cadre walked across the dirt floor and forced open the shutters. The afternoon shone directly onto the gray silk.

"That's them," he said pointing at the heap. "They don't smell as bad as they used to, but they still turn my gut."

The man, Comrade Houey, was one of those who had never learned the maxim of not saying anything at all if you have nothing positive to say. He was the provincial chief: the head communist honcho of Luang Prabang, and he had long since foregone politeness and manners as a waste of good grumbling time. Siri disliked his type.

"How long have they been here?"

"Couple of days."

Siri leaned over and slowly started to unwrap the bullet-holed tarpaulin. Inside, two carbonized corpses were slotted together in fetal position. He looked up at the fat man whose brow was permanently scowling.

"Thanks for taking such good care of them."

"Good care? What do they want, coffee and room service?" He laughed at his own sarcasm.

"You could have made some effort to keep them separate. If you really wanted an accurate autopsy, you should have—"

"Just as well, then. I don't want an autopsy at all. You're here for one reason and one reason only. We just want to know where these bastards come from."

Siri lowered his head and looked up at the man through the mat of his eyebrows. "You surely don't mean their nationality?"

"I certainly do. They told me in Vientiane you were some tit-hot genius when it came to solving puzzles. Well, here's a puzzle. Solve it."

"Now, wait. It isn't as easy as that. How the hell am I supposed to know where they came from?"

"You're the expert."

"I can probably tell you what killed them, but..."

"Doesn't take a genius to tell that. Look at 'em. It wasn't bloody lung cancer. Just get on with it." He turned and walked to the door.

"Hey."

"What?"

The man stopped and looked back.

"Where am I supposed to look at them?"

"What? You don't like a little bit of dirt? Just put some of those newspapers down if you're afraid of getting your nice white coat dirty."

Siri was an amazingly calm man. If he ever raised his voice, it was generally a deliberate ploy for the benefit of the misguided person in front of him. He considered it his duty to teach good manners to those whose parents had omitted doing so. He took a deep breath.

"You will find me a clean room—"

"I'll do no such thing."

"—and if you interrupt me again, I promise you'll be very sorry."

This was a showdown. The man's alcohol-suffused pores began to turn his bloated face the color of a gibbon's backside.

"Who do you—?"

"You'll find me a clean room with a table and—"

The man was fit to burst. He trembled. It was obvious he'd never been spoken back to.

"Don't . . . don't you know who I am?"

"'Who' doesn't matter. I know *what* you are. And what you are is rude. From now on, I shall tell you exactly what I need, and you'll arrange it for me. Perhaps it's you who don't know who *I* am, or who I have lunch with every day. I am the national coroner, and as such I deserve more respect than you've shown so far. Off with you, and find me a room."

Siri sat on the pile of books beside the corpses and folded his arms. He could see indecision on the fat man's face mixed with rage, yet Houey tried one final volley.

"You'll be sorry for this. I'll—"

Siri stood up very quickly and stepped toward him. There was no intent of malice, but the man saw it as an attack and hurtled himself out of the shed and across the yard. Siri stood in the doorway and watched him go. He knew the district chief would return with either a loaded pistol or news of a vacant room. He hoped the reference to his lunch companion was enough to make it the latter.

The room had once been a kitchen, but there was a large tiled concrete slab in the center that was ideal for the autopsy.

Siri was alone in there. The two corpses were so crisp, there were unlikely to be any delicate organs to weigh, or stomach contents to analyze. There certainly wasn't going to be a national emblem tattooed anywhere.

He wrote his observations in a notebook. From the breadth of the skulls, Siri was certain these were males. The smell told him they'd been engulfed in a petroleum fire. It had been intense enough to cremate them rapidly. They had assumed the same attitude, one that suggested they'd been in a sitting position when the flames first hit them. There was no trace left of their feet.

Remarkably, although their bodies and faces had been reduced to carbon, the top quarters of their heads were comparatively unscathed. Their hair was singed but in place, and a line of skin, free of soot, followed the hairline of each man.

With a blunt scalpel, he began to probe at the outer layers that were now a fusion of skin and clothing. With no microscope and no laboratory he'd have to get samples from various locations to take back to Vientiane before he could be absolutely sure of what he was seeing. In the meantime he had to trust his nose. The scent of burned leather was oddly distinct from that of burned skin. He found traces of it at the truncated ankles and at the waists.

This suggested to him that both men had been wearing high-top leather boots and belts. If he ever got to the site of the fire, he'd probably find buckles there to confirm his theory. He also discovered traces of some thick synthetic material welded to the left shoulder and chest of one man and the right shoulder and chest of the other.

He was about to cut into the bodies when he was disturbed by a light tap at the door.

"Come in."

The door opened slightly and a middle-aged woman with a pleasant face and long healthy hair put her head through the gap. She was deliberate in not looking in the direction of Siri or the bodies.

"Dr. Siri. I'm Latsamy. Comrade Houey has assigned me to take care of you while you're here."

Siri melted at the sound of her musical Luang Prabang dialect. There was no tune more erotic in the whole of Laos than the spoken song of a Luang Prabang girl. "Do you need anything?" she asked.

"Perhaps you could just stand here and talk to me for a few hours."

It was unlikely. She still wasn't able to turn her head in the direction of the corpses.

"I would like to avoid such a thing if I could, uncle."

"Am I that unpleasant?"

"Not you, uncle, them. I'd be as sick as a vomit bird if I had to look at those things. I don't know how you can do it. Would you like some tea or anything?"

"Tea would be very nice, thank you."

Once the door was closed, he reproached himself for flirting. He was old enough to know better. He knew he was a harmless old codger, but he'd probably frightened the girl.

He returned his attention to the bodies. Cutting into them was like retrieving baked roots from an earthen kiln. The heat had done a thorough job of overcooking everything. The angle of the pelvic indentation and the narrow sacrum confirmed that these were male. From the lengths of the femurs he assumed they were of small stature, more likely Asian than Caucasian.

He used a chisel to force open the jaws. The upper incisors curved into the shape of a shovel. This single fact put them into the Mongolian category. There was over an eighty-percent chance that these two poor gentlemen had been Asian. Either that, or they were Finnish. That was as close as he was ever likely to get to establishing their nationality. There was no fancy foreign dental work, no rings or bracelets, and they weren't talking: not yet, anyway.

It was while he was digging around in one lower abdomen that his tea arrived. It slid in on a chair between the open door and its frame without a word from the server. Siri was about to take a tea break when his scalpel struck metal. It had been his intention to use his cheat list at the back of his notebook to estimate the age of the men from wear and tear on their pelvic bones. But the bullet proved far more interesting.

It was wedged against the pubic crest. Tracing its trajectory was a complex and delicate matter. The damage the bullet had caused was well hidden by the contraction of the muscles. But as he slowly worked his way south, he came across a second bullet, then, at the anus, a third. The bullets had almost certainly entered the body from below.

Inspired by this discovery, he checked the other body and found two bullets. They were higher, almost at the base of the rib cage, but they too had entered from below. All these incidental clues tripped over one another on their way to one conclusion.

He sat on the chair by the door and drank his cold tea. The bodies, like dismembered model kits, sat on the slab looking back at him. He doubted, from the attitude of his host, whether these two would be getting any kind of funeral service. But he still wanted to put them back together, make them look respectable. He had a feeling they'd be back.

By the time his work was complete, it was already mid-afternoon. It had been a long day, and he was exhausted. He poked his head out of the room and found the lovely Miss Latsamy embroidering the hem of a traditional Lao skirt. She was very adept, and Siri thought she would make a fine surgeon—as long as she didn't have to look at the bodies.

"Miss Latsamy." He joined her in the vestibule. "I have three favors to ask."

"I was told to give you whatever you want." She blushed at how that came out.

"Good. Then first, I'd like you to go to the least political temple you can think of in Luang Prabang and tell the abbot that we have two bodies here that would very much like to be buried. As the deaths were violent, there probably won't be a cremation ceremony until the spirits are settled, but it would be nice if they could be buried on temple ground."

"Yes, uncle."

"Secondly, I have to go to a place called Pak Xang this afternoon."

"Oh."

"Oh, what?"

"Comrade Houey said you'd be going back to Vientiane this afternoon. The helicopter's waiting."

"Comrade Houey made a mistake. I have some business of my own here. I'll be going back tomorrow. Do you think you can find me some transport to Pak Xang?"

"I'll see what I can do."

"And I suppose it's time for me to report to the comrade about my findings. It would probably be better if he came here so I could show him what I've got. But it's up to him. Wherever we are, I doubt he'll be very happy with what I have to say."

"He never is."

"I see that."

"Asian? Damned Asian? Is that the best you can do?" The district chief had come to the room with a short blunt man who seemed to be some type of bodyguard. He nodded aggressively at the end of each utterance that passed the boss's lips.

"Yes."

"Well, that isn't good enough. It takes you three hours and all you discover is that these two could be from anywhere?"

"In Asia, yes."

"Some genius you turned out to be."

"There is one other thing."

"What?"

"Tomorrow morning I need to go and see the crash site."

"Well, you can't. . . . *What* crash site?"

"Where the helicopter came down. These two were pilots."

"Who the hell told you?"

"They did."

"Eh? Well, you're wrong. Totally wrong."

"Am I? Let's look at the facts. They were burned in a sitting position. They wore uniforms. Originally they were wearing helmets but I assume your rescue team helped themselves to souvenirs."

"How could you . . . ?"

"They were strapped in with seat belts and couldn't get away from the fire. The blast at their feet was extreme and the flames spread so fast, I'm assuming they were covered in fuel from the explosion. That tells me they were carrying a lot of spare gas in the cockpit, which in turn makes me think they expected to be traveling a long distance or carrying a lot of weight.

"And of course, the fact that they'd both been shot a number of times didn't give them much of a chance of getting out of the burning chopper. The closeness and angle of the bullets suggest they weren't traveling very fast. That's why I'm assuming it was a helicopter rather than a plane. I've retrieved the bullets, all AK47, LPLA issue. So whoever these two gentlemen were, they were probably gunned down by our people. How am I doing?"

Houey looked at the nodding guard and laughed. The man laughed nervously back.

"Our visiting genius from the capital has been doing a lot of guessing. Too bad he isn't much of a guesser." He turned to Siri. "No, comrade. You're wrong."

"I don't think so."

Houey huffed, and the two men left the room without further comment.

Miss Latsamy stepped into the doorway after they'd gone. Staring at the window, she said "uncle, can you ride a horse?"

It was barely a horse. It was more a pony with a paunch. But Siri had ridden many such creatures in his time in the mountains. Indeed, he quite relished the thought of returning to the saddle. Pak Xang was about fifteen kilometers from Luang Prabang, a distance he used to cover regularly between villages in his days with the Viet Minh.

But the old Lao saying "A year away from the nipple can make a baby nauseous of breast milk" was coined neither for fun nor for scholastic debate. His motorcycle saddle had made him soft. Five kilometers out of town, he negotiated the animal out of its happy canter and into a more leisurely trot. Old dears on bicycles with huge bundles of lemon grass overtook him. The journey took ninety minutes, not much faster than if he and the animal had changed places.

Forbidden Fruit

Still sore, Siri walked away from his sister-in-law's simple house feeling even sadder than when he had arrived. Everything about Wilaiwan reminded him of his wife. The way she smiled, her walk, even the widow's peak that stood on her forehead like the prow of a great white ship.

The sisters had been born nine months apart: yield from the sibling production line so common in well-off families of the old regime. Boua, his wife, had been the middle child of nine and the only rebel. While her family was in the royal capital working under the king's patronage, Boua was in France training to overthrow the royal family and rescue her country for communism.

She had returned to Laos after eight years, with ideals and a rather baffled doctor husband called Siri. But she never came back to Luang Prabang. Instead, she dragged her lover through the jungles of Vietnam and northern Laos and joined the Pathet Lao in their struggle against tyranny.

Now she was dead, and Siri had come to let her sister know how she had lain on a grenade and pulled the pin to end the confused misery that haunted the final years of her life. In some way, she had expected to erase the depression that had infected her and then spread to her sad husband.

But, of course, he didn't tell her. How could he? Honesty can be a dirty gift. It can muddy a sparkling stream of memories. So he said there had been a raid. She'd died a brave patriot as she'd lived, full of hope for a new regime.

Wilaiwan received the news passively and silently, and together they'd sat on the old wicker chairs on the veranda and let tears roll down their faces without embarrassment.

As there wasn't but an hour of daylight left, she invited him to stay the night. Her husband had caught two juicy catfish that were keen to be eaten with some homemade rice wine. So Siri went for a walk to build up an appetite and a better mood.

He crossed the dusty intersection that marked the center of the village and found the riverbank. There, he followed a river, creamy brown like slow-moving café au lait. He stepped carefully to avoid setting off the dog fart flowers. The setting sun seemed to walk along the opposite bank, dodging between the trees. Toward Luang Prabang, stodgy hills were patchy with slashed fields that looked from a distance like painful skin grafts.

Although there was no fence to announce it, he soon found himself in a fruit orchard. A longboat was moored against a simple wooden dock. The trees were neatly ranked but showing the effects of neglect. They were swollen with fruit. Some had rotted and dropped to the grass below. The sight may not have caused a flicker of interest to any other traveler, but to Siri it was uncanny. It baffled him that there were no signs of bird or insect damage. No animals had come to steal the luscious fallen oranges or nibble at the low-hanging pears. He walked along the rows; mangosteens, rambutans, rose apples, all proudly ripe and unviolated. It was astounding. Apparently, not even man, the most insatiable predator of all, had been scrounging from this Garden of Eden.

There was a feeling there. Not his usual creepy "somebody dead hanging around" feeling, but an aura of sorts: a protection, as if something were watching over the trees and the spirits that resided in them. He felt safe under its gaze.

He was curious to know where he was and to learn more about the exotic strains of fruit, many of which he'd never seen before. He walked up and down the lush green rows. They'd have needed three or four waterings a day through this particularly dry summer season to keep them so bountiful. It wasn't till his last sweep that he came upon a gardener.

The old man wore a conical Vietnamese hat tied under his chin with a bright red cloth. He had on a navy blue peasant's jacket and shorts. He stood inside the canopy of an orange tree, pruning up into the branches. Siri couldn't make out much of his looks.

"Good health, friend," Siri began.

The man didn't interrupt his work to reply. "How would you be, friend?"

"You have some remarkable fruit trees here."

"Thank you. I'm afraid they've been neglected of late. I haven't been able to get out here for some time."

The man's voice was soft, somehow worldly and, Siri thought, kind. He guessed he was around his own age.

"I don't seem to recognize a lot of these varieties."

"No? Know fruit, do you?"

"Most of the jungle types, and the usual imports."

"Well, you wouldn't have seen a lot of these. If you've got a few minutes, grab those pruning clippers and give me a hand to cut back some branches. They won't get a lot of attention from now on."

"That's a shame. Why not?"

Either the man didn't answer or Siri couldn't hear through the foliage. He looked in the basket, where he found an elegant pair of pruning clippers and a beautifully gilded set of shears in the shape of herons necking.

"You take your gardening seriously."

"It isn't something you can half do."

Siri went to the orange tree beside his friend's and started on the old, low branches.

"It's peaceful here. How come you haven't been able to come?"

"It's the new regime, Brother. They're very strict here in Luang Prabang. They don't like us moving around too much."

"But this is a thriving orchard. It needs someone to look after it. You could feed a battalion of soldiers just from the produce here. You could certainly keep the villagers nearby alive."

The old man stopped clipping. "Hmm. Could do, I suppose. Except the people in these parts are somewhat loath to sample the fruits from this particular garden."

"Why's that?"

"I take it you aren't from around here."

"No. I'm part of the invading hordes. Spent most of my troubled life in the jungles of Houaphan and North Vietnam."

"Ah. You're one of them. That explains it. Then you wouldn't know whose orchard this is." There was a pause. "It belongs to the Royal Family, or what's left of it."

"All right. Then that might explain why the people aren't stealing His M's tasty fruits. But I don't really see how it keeps the birds and the bugs away."

"Ah, yes. Very observant of you. That is a little harder to explain."

He moved out from his tree and went to the next in the row after Siri's. Through the leaves, the doctor saw him in patches. He had a slow, somewhat pained gait but kept his back straight. He had the bearing of a royal gardener. No doubt about it. Siri could almost feel the old fellow's pride at tending such fine trees. It seemed cruel for the Party to keep him away from a job he loved.

Once he'd entered the next orange-leaf umbrella, the man said "I don't know if you've noticed, friend, but Luang Prabang is rather a magical place. There are many stories I could tell you."

The sun had given up hope, and Siri was aware he had a walk ahead of him in the dark. He lowered the clippers and sighed. "How did you get here, old fellow?"

"Boat."

"Do you suppose they'll let you come back tomorrow?"

"No. This is the end."

He made it sound like something other than a ban on gardening. If this were really his last visit, this pruning would seem to be more an act of desperation—or rebellion. Siri came out of his blackening hood of leaves and stood in the open. A large moon was already in the ascent.

"Then are you going back to town tonight?"

"Why do you ask?"

"I have to go to my sister-in-law's for dinner. But I'd be very interested to hear your stories. Couldn't you stay here tonight and go back in the morning?"

"It would upset an awful lot of people," the old man laughed. "But I suppose I could. A raspberry to them all."

Still, he hadn't emerged from his own shroud of oranges.

"That's good. Listen. I'll see what food I can rescue. You must be hungry. Maybe a bottle of rice whiskey? How does that sound?"

The clipping stopped. "That's very kind of you. Yes, very kind. I'll be here. Look for the fire."

The gardener's hand reached out through the leaves as if it belonged to the tree itself. The wrist was white with a thick wad of tied strings. The hand was blistered from the day's exertions. Siri shook it and felt a sudden stab of sadness. This was a man at the end of hope. He needed cheering up.

Farewell the Women's Unionist

It was about this time, probably as Siri was passing through the village on his way to Wilaiwan's house, that primary school teacher Chanmee was riding her bicycle along Khouvieng. The old bull testicle trees arched over the lane and blocked the moonlight. Without lamps, it was only her white blouse that gave her any substance on that dark stretch of road.

She hated traveling in the dark, but Wednesday was the meeting of her branch of the Lao Women's Union. She had to attend. This was always a scary journey for her. At times, a car's headlights would illuminate her way briefly, then plunge everything back into darkness.

She was straining her tired eyes for tree roots and potholes. No cars had passed for several minutes, and the street was so black that she decided to climb down from the bike and walk beside it. It was eerily quiet on that stretch, and the squeak from her front wheel was her only comfort.

Then there was the other sound. It came from behind her, somewhere off in the frangipani bushes. She stopped for a second to listen. It was a deep, steady growl like a painful snore. She assumed it to be a dog and wondered if it was injured. She'd never experienced any hostility from dogs, yet there was something sinister about this sound. It worried her enough to make her climb back on the bike.

The bushes rustled and a twig snapped, and she pushed down hard and too hastily on the pedal to try to build up some speed. The tightness of her *phasin* skirt restricted her movement, and her shoe slid from the pedal. The bicycle veered to the right and dipped into a deep rut. She overbalanced sideways.

Too slow to right herself, she tumbled onto the hard earth verge, the bicycle with her. She held her breath to listen for the growl. She looked around at the shadows. Nothing moved. Nothing made a sound. She laughed out loud at her foolishness.

She untangled herself from the bike and was about to get to her feet when the creature was on her. The huge first bite muted her scream. Blood soaked quickly into the white blouse. In less than thirty seconds she was dead.

Garden of Earthly Delights

Two hours later, Siri was back at the orchard. His hosts were early sleepers, unused to company. In his sack he had two bottles of earthy rice whiskey, the remains of the river fish, and a container of sticky rice. This would be a fitting last meal for a man who loved his vocation.

The moon had lit his path from, and back to, the orchard, like a lighthouse beacon guiding a foreign ship. He walked the aisles of fruit trees, breathing in their sweet nighttime scents. A blind man could have identified each tree.

The gardener had abandoned his futile task and was sitting between Siri and a blazing fire. A good pile of lopped branches was at his side, and the smoke carried the scent of the trees they came from. The man was stockier than he'd appeared earlier, and he hunched forward slightly as he stared at the flames.

Siri announced his arrival. "Good health, friend."

"Welcome back."

Siri put his aid package on the ground in front of the old man and the bottles clinked together as he pulled them from the sack.

"This should soften the pain of saying goodbye to your friends here, eh?"

He chuckled and turned to the old man. It was his intention to shake his hand to re-launch their friendship. But as he moved out of the line of the fire, the flames lit up the hooded eyes of the gardener. Siri froze. His own face must have reflected his shocked disbelief at what he was seeing.

The firelight shone directly onto the man's wide round features. The mouth spread slowly into a broad smile of neat teeth. It wasn't a face Siri had seen in the flesh, but it was one he knew only too well. It was a face he'd seen on 8mm film in the caves of Houaphan, accompanied by the jeers and laughter of the cadres. It was a face he'd carried to the market, folded in his shoulder bag. It was a face on propaganda posters they'd used in hate sessions at endless political seminars.

The man spoke through his smile. "I hope this doesn't disqualify me from having a drink."

"It isn't Dom Perignon."

"Thank goodness for that."

The king, into his second year of unemployment, leaned forward to shake the hand Siri had misplaced somewhere between them. "My name's—"

"Yeah. I know. Bugger me. This is one for the books. I'm Siri, Siri Paiboun. Am I supposed to . . . I don't know . . . curtsy or something?"

"I doubt that would do either of us any good. For heaven's sake, sit down and open a bottle."

Siri did as he was decreed, but he couldn't help laughing at the weirdness of the moment. He poured the whiskey into two half-coconut shells and handed one to the old man.

"What exactly are you doing here?" Siri asked.

"Bidding, as you rightly say, farewell to my trees. This is the place I'll miss most. Good health."

He gestured the coconut shell toward his guest, then took a swig. Siri was already aware of just how awful the homemade brew was, but the king showed no reaction to it.

"Good health." Siri drank and winced. "Yecch. I reckon we could piss this out as weed killer by the end of the night."

They both laughed.

"What brings you here, Comrade Siri?"

"Some mysterious emergency. I'm the national coroner, for want of a better one. They asked me to identify a couple of crispy fliers. The local Party head expected me to tell him their names and addresses. In return, he wasn't prepared to tell me a damn thing."

"I think you'll find they're both Lao royalists."

"What do you know?"

"There was an attempt, the day before yesterday, to take my family and me out of the country. One of the helicopters was shot down. I imagine that's where your fliers are from. I'm sure your LPLA people would like to confirm that they had connections to the old Royal Lao Government. The helicopter crashed in the grounds of That Luang temple. You should go and take a look there."

"Is that why you're leaving?"

"They want me somewhere less accessible from Thailand."

"You seem to be taking it all remarkably calmly."

"I'm resigned to it. It's been coming for some time."

"Since the abdication?"

"Long before that, I'm afraid. Our royal line has lost its *kwun*."

Even born-again-agnostic Siri was shocked to hear such a statement. Lao tradition had it that all living beings were in possession of a *kwun:* something between a soul and a spirit. Humans were said to have thirty-two *kwun*. In times of bad fortune, some of the *kwun* may flee, and shamans are called in to invite them to return. Only in serious illness or death does the *kwun* desert its host completely.

Siri looked at the man's wrists, heavy with loops of unspun white thread. When begging the *kwun* to return, it was usual to circle the wrists of the unlucky one with strings and knot them. Somebody close to the king had been doing some serious negotiating with the spirit world.

"You really believe that?"

"There's no doubt."

"When did it happen?" He refilled the coconut shells.

"When I came along."

"Now, you're just being hard on yourself."

"It's a fact. Indisputable. In my father's time, he and my uncle, Phetsarath, were in harmony with the spirits. This orchard was theirs. Are you sensitive to necromancy, Dr. Siri?"

"I'm afraid I am."

"Then you can probably feel the spirits of the trees here and the hold they have over this region. I'm told it's very strong. I cannot feel it myself. The whole of Luang Prabang is evidently bristling with the ghosts of previous kings and queens and their offspring. There's been a magical connection between the Royal Capital and the occult since the days of my great ancestor, King Fa Ngum. It was he who brought the first spirits to this place. He had thirty-three teeth, you know?"

"He what?"

"Thirty-three teeth. It's almost unheard of. The Lord Buddha also had thirty-three, and although he never mentioned it, the dental records showed that my uncle had thirty-three teeth as well. It's a sign, an indication that you've been born as a bridge to the spirit world."

"And you believe all this?" Siri asked as he began to use his tongue to count the teeth in his own mouth.

"There's been too much evidence to doubt it." Siri noticed for the first time that a cricket had come to rest on the old king's shoulder. "Do you recall that your Viet Minh friends tried to invade Luang Prabang in the early fifties?"

"Yes." Siri lost count of his teeth.

"What reason did they give for their failure?"

"Hmm, let me think. Something about the place being heavily fortified and manned with well-armed French militia."

"Ha. So I thought. The French didn't get here in time. All we had was a handful of old retainers with rusty hunting rifles. A crochet society could have invaded us. The advisers told my father we were doomed and that he should flee.

"But he stayed. That night, he gathered the shamans, and they called on the spirits to protect the capital. The following day, the Viet Minh were advancing upon us. They were so cocksure, they were already divvying up the spoils as they marched. But suddenly they began to fall."

"In what way?"

"Just drop. A number were taken by some mysterious palsy. They lost all their strength. Their eyes rolled in their sockets and they couldn't speak. More and more fell to this mysterious disease, until the commanders called a halt to the advance. They had to drag the stricken men back on bamboo travoises.

"Their medics couldn't fathom what ailment had struck them down or how to treat them. But the next day, they awoke, right as rain. So they came at us again. And the same thing happened."

"I admit, I didn't hear that version. I would have remembered it if I had."

"You don't believe it?"

"Over the last six months, I've started to believe almost everything."

"In my uncle's case, I saw it for myself. We would spend a day with him in Luang Prabang, then someone would arrive from Vientiane and tell you he'd spent the same day with him there. He could be at two or three places at once. On one occasion, I saw him rise from the ground. He just levitated."

"Ah, so this isn't the first time you've tried my sister-in-law's homemade rice whiskey?"

They both laughed.

"But, Dr. Siri, I don't have any of these gifts. When I was born, the shamans predicted that the *kwun* would leave the royal line along with me, that I wouldn't live out my reign. When my father died, I knew I didn't have the power to hold on to the magic that had helped us survive for so many centuries."

Siri shook his head. "No. This is history, my friend. A revolution has nothing to do with appeasing the spirits. You're a victim of politics, not destiny."

"I agree that there are semantics involved. Even from the practical point of view, I have little leverage. My supporters have all fled. I have two confidants that I would trust with my life, but most of the entourage gave us lip service until they knew our fate. If my father were here, the *kwun* would show him the way to overcome your politics. It hasn't shown me. I'm told it's getting weaker day by day. When they move us from Luang Prabang, the connection will be severed. Our will cannot survive a move."

"Ah. Don't be so cheerful. They'll just put you up in a camp for a few months, give you some Marxist propaganda to memorize, then bring you back a new improved born-again commie royal. They'll hold you up as an example for the masses."

"There will be no coming back."

"Now, why do you have to talk like that?"

"You're right. I'm sorry. Let's speak of more delightful things—to counteract the bitter agony of this paint thinner we're drinking."

"Thank God for that. I was starting to think you were actually enjoying the stuff."

"May I ask how your revolution's going?"

"Revolutions always go more smoothly around a campfire in the jungle than they do in real life."

"You'll forgive me if I say you don't come across as a hardened socialist."

"It's a bit of an anticlimax."

"I understand. I heard your prime minister's inspirational speech on the radio. I think the expression he used was 'no major achievements in the first year of office.' I was sure he could have found one little thing to boast about."

"I think the takeover took us all by surprise. It happened so suddenly."

"Twenty years is hardly sudden," remarked the king.

"Ah, but that's just it. All the sitting around tends to make you stodgy and lethargic. You get to wonder whether your revolutionary dream will ever come true. Then—poof—there you are running a country. The PL was swept into power in Laos on the back of the angry North Vietnamese dragon."

"You've always held on to its tail."

"That's true. But I believe we're a more gentle version."

"The hundred thousand people that fled across the river didn't appear to think so."

"They were running away from the unknown rather than the reality. We're quite sweet, really."

The king sipped at the whiskey and turned the natural grimace it produced into a wry smile. "So you haven't been sending officials from the old regime to concentration camps?"

"I think the Party refers to them as re-education camps. They're like holiday camps with barbed wire and hard labor. Look, I know what you're saying. I share some of your concerns. I don't like locking people up for their beliefs. But I also understand that—at least in these early days—there's a need for stability. The LPRP can't afford to have vocal dissent stirring up anti-government feeling. They've got enough problems without that."

"But—"

"And you have to admit that your old government officials and military and police weren't exactly angels of purity. The Security Council's been uncovering evidence of unbelievable corruption all the way up the ladder."

"I'm sure it won't take your new officials long to master the fine art of graft. Greed is sadly inherent in the soul of man."

"Again, I agree. But we do have a lot of good people. They really have the well-being of Laos at heart. You don't spend half your adult life in caves if your intention is to make yourself wealthy. They may not be popular in the towns, but let's not forget that eighty-five percent of the population works the land. With all due respect, the old regime pretty much let them get on with it. You bought their products at a fraction of market value and didn't do a thing to help them through droughts and epidemics."

"And your communist brothers and sisters will."

"I think they'll try."

"Then let us thank the Lord Buddha for that."

Even while his words were still floating there in the air, Siri wondered whether he really believed what he'd just said. So many of those jungle dreams seemed to evaporate when exposed to reality. Once the cadres moved into the cities, the shoes of the old regime began to fit them quite well. There was already a rumor that officials at the Agricultural Ministry were taking kickbacks and rerouting seed stocks.

When he was at the temple in Savanaketh, Siri had read a translation of *Animal Farm* as a French primer. He had thought it was a story about animals on a farm. It wasn't until it was condemned by the Communist Party in Paris as capitalist propaganda that he read it again as a political statement. He was starting to recognize some of the beasts.

Time passed quickly, and the two old men discussed Orwell and Voltaire, Engels and Guizot and Vailland, Césaire, spiraling down to Simenon and Hergé, wisely veering away from politics as the liquor slowly took hold.

In one of their last moments of sober clarity, Siri and the king had the brilliant idea of mixing Wilaiwan's lethal brew with the juice of some succulent fruits from the orchard. The result was an ideal aperitif to accompany the fish and the rice, and the perfect antidote to depression.

When the whiskey bottles were empty, the two men lay side by side on a mat of lush grass, exhausted from a final bout of laughter, invigorated by talk of literature and music, at peace and at one with the aromatic fruit. There, Siri watched the cricket on the king's shoulder, licking its fingernails, and he slowly joined the old regent in sleep.

As the spirits resided in the trees, and the fruit grew on those trees and that fruit was now inside Siri, it was no surprise that his sleep should be filled with the light and color of a spectacular dream.

It was day. He was in the orchard, but the orchard was enormous. The trees stretched far into the sky. The tree spirits were everywhere, dancing, singing, having a thoroughly good time. It was an animated Hieronymus Bosch scene similar to the one he'd seen in a visiting exhibition at the Louvre in Paris. In fact, it was exactly that scene, except all the participants were Lao and not quite as naked.

Male angels juggled ripe oranges that had once been the breasts of the nymphs who cheered them on. The grand old dowager, Lady Tani, strummed on her Lao harp beside her dazzling yellow banana tree. Gooseberry sprites performed aerobatics. The whispering ghosts moved from spirit to spirit, telling them their futures and collecting star fruits as payment.

Siri and the king sat cross-legged beneath a mulberry fig tree, watching the extravaganza around them. Banyan tree angels stood guard behind them. His Majesty was in full white ceremonial garb, and medals glittered like treasure on his chest. A footman with a straggly gray beard dangling from the point of his chin stood a pace back from him.

Cicadas sang in tune like a choir. Color-coordinated butterflies circled in swarms so dense, they changed the hue of the sky at will. The footman announced the arrival of guests, and the king looked to Siri to see if he approved. The doctor raised an eyebrow and waved his hand. It was a gesture he remembered from the bald king in the Hollywood film that had insulted Siam and thus delighted the Pathet Lao.

"Etcetera, etcetera, etcetera," he said, for no other reason than it was the only line he remembered from that picture show.

The footman returned with two handsomely hobbling pilots who, due to the absence of feet, carried their expensive leather boots under their arms. They were Lao and they greeted their king in royal language.

"Sire, we shall try once more."

"We were betrayed, Lord. They were expecting us. There is a traitor in your camp."

With that, the footman exploded horribly, bits of him flying in all directions. Siri looked around to see whether there were accusing eyes pointed at him. But suddenly there were no eyes to point. When he looked back, the king was gone. All that remained was a plate of crispy fried crickets and a side dip.

The pilots were standing back to back as if primed for an attack. The cowardly spirits were retreating to their trees, blending into the bark, merging with the branches, sinking into the roots. A wind rose, rustling the leaves. It grew until it began to shake the succulent fruits from the trees.

Left were Siri and the two pilots in a storm-darkened vignette. One pilot turned to him and nodded. "We are grateful."

And with that, the two men burst into flames, burned to ash, and were blown away by the frantic wind. The tree leaves all around flapped in panic, as if in the grip of a monsoon. Alone, Siri listened to a roar of distant thunder, a roar of a beast, the gnar of terror. Toward the south, the trees were bending as if to clear the path of the creature that owned the terrible roar. The sky was black now, and Siri tensed for the storm.

He was learning to be an observer in his own dreams. Years before, he had felt obliged to be a participant; he'd played the roles and assumed the appropriate emotions. But now he watched them like a man in the front row of an empty cinema. He convinced himself that he wouldn't be killed by the villain or truly loved by the heroines.

But something about the sound of the creature there that crashed through the jungle was a warning to him. This was beyond a dream, too real. It was a sign that he should expect to hear this sound in his waking hours and that it would be a critical moment. He knew somehow that he had to be aware of this sound because it had connections to the killings in Vientiane and could signal the end of him.

And he awoke, or perhaps he didn't, and he was in a box. It was black and musty and he could see nothing, but he knew he was in a box. Logically he assumed it was that final box, that he had succumbed to that incontrovertible last argument with nature. But no.

He smelled the smoke of a cheap cigarette. He felt the warm spray of something mildly caustic against his face. It smelled of liquor. There was a creak, and the lid of the box opened and light rushed in on him. Faces looked down at him: blanched, unemotional faces. Some had lips the color of a new wound; some wore jewels that neither glittered nor suggested wealth; all had empty black two-dimensional eyes that tapered to lizard tails.

Siri was small and shrunken, as if he were their toy. He looked up. They looked down. There were no sounds. For the longest time they stared up and down at each other, until the lid of the box slowly closed and Siri was back in the musty dark. But he had committed their faces to memory.

When the actual morning brought its actual awakening, Siri was disoriented and alone. The scents of the heavy fruits were still all around him, but they seemed overly sweet, offering a final advertisement of their ripeness before all was lost. The feeling of being protected was gone. He heard the scurrying of animals and saw briefly a marmot carrying off a ripe orange in its mouth. The branches buzzed with insects.

He turned to his side and saw the indentation of the king, like a cartoon accident in the thick grass. In the dip where the head had lain, the cricket from the king's shoulder lay dry and lifeless. Lao tradition had it that the *kwun* materialized in the form of a cricket. If that was true, the king had been right: the *kwun* had left him.

999,999 Elephants

Siri went to bid goodbye to his sister-in-law and her husband, who were already toiling in the rice field. They were making their contribution to the cooperative, which allowed them to work one small corner of the land they had once owned. It was the land Wilaiwan had been awarded as a senior court dancer. The royal seal on her document meant no more now than her bourgeois skills.

"Thank you for loving my sister," she said, pulling her saucer-shaped hat back from her eyes. She hadn't asked where he'd spent the night. She'd learned not to ask too many questions, even of a relative. He'd already decided against telling her of his visit with the king. It would have been too distressing for a royalist to hear of the loss of the royal *kwun*.

"It was my pleasure, and that's the truth of it."

"I'm glad she had you."

"Wan, I have a small mystery I'm trying to solve."

"I doubt I could help with the type of mystery you're engaged in."

"I'm not so sure. In Vientiane, there's a teak chest with a royal seal. It's about the size of a child's coffin. It doesn't have any keyhole or handle, and it seems impossible to open. I believe there's some great force inside."

"I'm sure there are many such chests of looted royal treasures in Vientiane." She bit her tongue.

"I've imagined faces," he continued, "white unemotional

faces with extreme makeup and elaborate headgear. There's also some connection with tobacco smoke and alcohol." Her face showed some recognition. "Does that remind you of something?"

"In Luang Prabang, in a house on Kitsalat near the palace, is a man called Inthanet. Go and see him if you have a chance. He might be able to help."

The sun was rapidly burning through the morning mist that loitered along the river and the surrounding hills. The pony was still tethered to the front steps of the house, but Siri's groin ached from the previous day's journey. Much of his trip back to the city was beside, rather than on top of, the relieved little horse.

When they finally reached Luang Prabang, he returned the pony to Miss Latsamy's brother and repaid his kindness by lancing and treating a boil on his shoulder. He needed to remind himself occasionally that he still had the ability to solve the problems of the living.

He walked along Photisalat, past the squat two-story buildings squashed together like uneven books on a library shelf. Their bindings were all sunburned browns, dusty yellows and greens. A grandmother on one upstairs balcony smiled through a bloody betel-nut mouth when he winked at her.

He paused in front of the old Royal Palace, reluctantly donated to the State as a museum. Its tall lush palms still stood at attention beside the dirt drive. Above the portal, the same royal emblem he'd seen on the chest at the Information Ministry stood out in gold relief from a red background. It was partially masked by the new national flag but not yet defaced. He wondered where his gardener friend might be at that moment, whether he'd ever see the inside of his palace again.

He would seek out Mr. Inthanet, but not yet. He walked away from the modest downtown, and trees soon became more common than buildings. He stopped two monks in brown woolen hats and asked for directions to That Luang temple. They steered him there via lefts and rights at this type of tree and that type of bush. All the royal street signs had been taken down.

When he arrived at the whitewashed wall of the small temple, an armed guard at the gate stopped him by waving in his face.

"The temple's closed, comrade."

"Of course. I know," Siri said confidently. "I'm here to see the crash site. I'm from the Department of Justice in Vientiane."

"Oh."

Siri produced his foolscap ID. The boy didn't look much further than the letterhead, and the doctor wondered whether he could read.

"Nobody told me."

"Comrade Houey sent me."

"Oh."

Siri put his paper back into his cloth shoulder bag and walked past the guard as if everything had been sorted out. He gave the boy a friendly nod and went up the steps to the mound upon which Wat That Luang sat. At the top, the dry earth yard was shaded by lush old pagoda trees, and the temple buildings were quaint and sadly run down. There were no monks around. Siri could see that an area of the grounds had been cordoned off by a tall wall of blue plastic sheeting nailed to bamboo poles. He walked through the flap in the plastic, and an astonishing scene presented itself before him.

To one side, a trail of blackened debris gouged through the yard and settled at the crumpled and burned-out wreck of a helicopter. To the other, a large old elephant was harnessed to twelve meters of thick chain. The rusting metal looped down, then up, around the waist of a badly damaged black stupa that leaned sideways like the great Tower of Pisa.

Two mahouts were securing the chain to the elephant's sides. A man in a paper-thin white shirt stood pointing in the direction he intended the stupa to fall. Two more armed guards stood behind him. Siri walked confidently up to the man and smiled.

"It was damaged by the crash?"

The man turned but didn't seem all that surprised to see Siri. They shook hands, and the white-shirted man nodded toward the precarious relic.

"The helicopter apparently caught it as it was coming down. You from the town hall?"

"No. I'm the coroner. I've been working on the pilots. You aren't from around here?"

"I'm sent by the Buddhist Sangha Council. I just got in this morning on the bus. I'm here to supervise the demolition of this here stupa. It's dangerous like this. We wouldn't want it to fall on some little child, would we? All alterations to temple structures, be they as a result of planning or of acts of the Lord himself, have to be cleared by the Council."

It was one of those unnecessarily long answers you get from someone feeling guilty about something.

"This is quite a security force for such a little stupa."

"Well, there's the—how can I say it? There's the historical implication of this moment, and of course there's the danger of pillaging."

"Bricks?"

"Goodness, no. A lot of these very old stupas, particularly up here in the north, contain a good deal of"—he lowered his voice—"treasure. As you know, the slaves of capitalism often gain merit by donating large sums of gold and jewels to temples. In the olden days, the abbots used to keep their treasures safe from invading armies by entombing them within the structure of the stupa."

"Oh, I see."

Cynical, Siri wondered whether the Buddhist Council would have shown this enthusiasm if the helicopter had toppled a wall or a temple roof. But he gave the man the benefit of the doubt.

"Good luck."

He walked over to the crashed helicopter and used a spine of metal to ferret through the ashes. The fire had been hot enough to melt the windshield and parts of the fuselage. All that remained of the seats were the stubs of springs.

As he suspected, there was nothing new to be learned there. He found the melted clip of a seat belt, and slivers of tin around the site that were obviously from exploding petrol cans. Everything confirmed the findings from the autopsy. He just wanted to announce quietly to himself how clever he was. Being right can be a very satisfying experience.

Surprisingly, the craft wasn't armor-plated. There were several bullet holes in the fuselage, and it obviously wasn't a military vehicle. Siri assumed the pilots had invested all their hopes in getting in and out and away with the minimum of fuss. They certainly hadn't been expecting the barrage they got, and had had no defense against it. For some reason, the military had been expecting them.

Job done, he went back to the treasure hunt. The elephant was secured and one mahout was on its neck. The other stood behind, jabbing a large wooden spike into the animal's rear end. The links of the chain groaned and the crunch of four-hundred-year-old brickwork disturbed the previous silence of the temple. But still nothing, neither the elephant nor the stupa, showed any noticeable movement. It was a frieze with sound.

Siri stood behind the white-shirted official.

"You've probably noticed already. . . ."

"What's that, comrade?"

"The skid marks behind the helicopter."

The chain groaned once more. "Yes?"

"Well, if that were indeed the trajectory, and it does appear that it worked up a good head of speed before it stopped, I don't see how it could possibly have nicked your stupa on the way down."

The man's amicable nature seemed to retract like the head of a turtle. "Those were the official findings submitted in the official report from the Luang Prabang regional office, sir. They are far more knowledgeable than you or I on matters such as this. Surely you aren't suggesting this is a coincidence? What else could have caused it?"

"I'm certainly not a ballistics specialist, but that hole in the side of the stupa . . . just a guess, mind you, but if there were a mortar placement, say, at the base of Phousy Hill up there, and if it were taking potshots at the helicopter after it was already on its way down, it certainly could have caused a lot of damage."

The man was turning most indignant. "I hope you don't think one of our own people could be responsible for the destruction of this historic site."

Siri could tell this man was no kindred spirit. He smiled and looked ahead. "That elephant doesn't look too well."

The noble beast suddenly took one unexpected backward step and broke most of the bones in the foot of the man with the spike. It then wavered slightly, like a hot-air balloon in a thermal, and sank onto its front knees. In spite of the blasphemous yelling of the rear mahout, it managed a dignified death. It looked to either side for the most comfortable landing; then, like the good socialist slave it was, it leaned to its left.

The ground beneath Siri's feet shook when the elephant crashed onto the earth. The neck mahout leaped to the ground and ran to help his screaming friend. With not one more thought for the dying animal, he offered himself as a crutch and guided his colleague toward the gate.

Siri walked to the shallow-breathing elephant and knelt at its head. The mahouts he'd known in the jungle would mourn for days if they lost such a proud animal. But cities and mercenary cowboys were gradually destroying those bonds. They could replace an elephant like a flat tire. This animal deserved better: it deserved respect.

He lay his palm flat beside the animal's cloudy eye and whispered incantations still engraved on his memory from his days as a novice. The guards looked on in amazement.

"What's he doing?"

"Giving the thing its last rites, by the look of it."

"He must be nuts."

But Siri continued until he could no longer see his reflection in the milky iris. The eye no longer saw. The elephant no longer lived. And at that moment, a surge, like a massive overdose of Vietnamese coffee, passed through Siri's body. The breath was sucked from him, and his heart jived out of control in his chest. He knew right away that the spirit of the old beast had passed through him and that something undefinable had been left there. Even after his pulse slowed, he knew there was a difference about him.

He was distracted from his thoughts by the sound of crumbling masonry. Some reaction had been started by the elephant's tug-of-war. Old natural mortar was slowly turning to dust, and the clay bricks it once held secure were sliding from their housings, changing position.

Soon there was nothing to hold up the leaning structure, and the stupa flopped to the earth. It disintegrated inelegantly, as if it could never have stood up to the elements of centuries. There was very little noise; no trumpets or choirs, nothing grand to suggest that history had tumbled.

The official and his guards rushed over to the stupa's base, which stood square and hollow like an old wishing well. But their wishes were not to come true. Even before they started to scoop the wayward bricks from the base, they knew this was an empty stupa. The early enthusiasm of the guards gradually turned to languor, and after twenty minutes they showed no interest whatsoever in shoveling.

The official was left with nothing but professional obligation. He noted the time of the destruction for his report and wrapped one small brick in a sheet of newspaper to take back with him on the bus. He photographed the pile of bricks and the dead elephant. That meant more unnecessary paperwork. Siri was sitting in the shade of a nearby frangipani, still trying to count his teeth. Years of spice had numbed the tip of his tongue. Hard labor in the jungle had desensitized his fingertips.

"Nine hundred and ninety-nine thousand, nine hundred and ninety-nine," he said.

"What was that, comrade?"

"Well, if this is Lan Xang, home of the million elephants. . . ."

The official gave a polite chuckle.

"Yes. I see. Very droll." He replaced his papers in his plastic briefcase with the camera and the brick. "Excuse me. I have a bus to catch."

Siri had been offered a bus ticket back to Vientiane by the District Chief, which he had naturally refused. Nothing would possess him to make that spine-jarring journey. He would take the plane or wait for the helicopter. It didn't matter that it wasn't available. It didn't matter that it was off on some top-secret mission. It didn't matter if he did have to wait two more days. He was flying back, and that was final.

The guards had gone, and he was alone in the temple grounds. It was blissfully peaceful. The main sala was a simple white rectangular building, but he was fascinated by the beautiful carvings on the black hardwood doors. There was something mystical about the figures that played there: the angels, the *naga*, the children of old kings. He walked closer to look at the expressions on their faces. Each had the same troubled look. They gazed directly into Siri's eyes, and something about their fear told him "Beware."

He shrugged off the feeling that came over him and set about hunting for accommodation. The monks had been temporarily removed, and a perfectly good dormitory terrace stood empty behind the prayer chapel. Bedrolls were piled at the far end in pyramids. As he wouldn't be leaving that day, he could think of no better place to spend the night. He carried a mattress into the chapel and laid it out beneath the watchful gold eye of the Lord Buddha.

Siri found Miss Latsamy in the City Law Administration Office where she worked for three dollars a month. She was stamping official seals onto documents that stood in rectangular towers across her desk. She looked up when he came in.

"Ah. Hello, uncle."

"Hello, Miss Latsamy. I was hoping you could tell me where I might find Comrade Houey."

She looked up at the clock on the wall.

"I don't think you can. He's preparing for . . . for the . . ." she didn't know what to call it ". . . the thing."

"The thing?"

Miss Latsamy looked across at the lady at the desk opposite, who raised a well-crayoned eyebrow. She said nothing.

"It doesn't really have a name, I don't think, uncle. Comrade Houey called all the shamans to a meeting in the Town Hall. Anyone who refuses will be arrested. They all have to bring their paraphernalia with them, because there's going to be a . . ."

"A thing."

"Right."

"What time's the meeting?"

"Seven. But it's only for shamans."

"I wouldn't miss it for the world, Miss Latsamy. Don't you know I'm the embodiment of a thousand-and-fifty-year-old holy man from Khamuan?"

She eyed him up and down. "You don't look it."

"It's very kind of you to say so."

The Daughter That Lived

Teacher Chanmee arrived at the morgue early in the afternoon. She was there on the bed of a pickup truck when Dtui got back from lunch.

"Hot, isn't it?"

"Damned hot."

"This is for you, Mrs."

The hospital driver was keen to get a signature on his chit and offload the body.

"If you called me 'Miss,' I might think about it."

Mr. Geung arrived just as she was signing. He wheeled out the morgue trolley and took the new guest to the examination room. As he was preparing to slot her into the freezer, Dtui came up behind him and looked at the body.

"See that, Mr. Geung? Those marks are almost identical to the ones on Auntie See."

He continued to prepare the teacher for storage.

"Let . . . let's w . . . wait for the comrade doctor."

"Wouldn't you trust me to cut her up, pal?"

"Dr. Siri is a . . . a doctor."

"And what am I?"

"A girl."

"What about when I come back from four years' study in the Soviet Union with a coroner's certificate? Will I still be just a girl then?"

"No."

"Good."

"Then you . . . you . . . you'll be an old girl."

He kept his face straight for as long as was humanly possible, then snorted his laugh. She picked up the bone cleaver and chased him around the dissection table.

Dtui was the unbreakable one. She was the survivor of a litter of children who all left life before puberty. Had they lived, she would now have five brothers and five sisters. But they hadn't been as lucky or as hardy or as wily as she proved to be. She went beyond the point that had taken most of her siblings: the cross-roads where childbirth and death meet. Without the assistance of immunization, her body had fought off all the usual child-hood diseases, and the curse of accidents had passed over her roof to give grief to the next household.

Her mother, Manoluk, had invested eleven lives of love into her surviving daughter. When her soldier husband was lost in one more meaningless battle, she brought her to Vientiane. Here she cooked and cleaned and washed for strangers and pushed Dtui through school. It wasn't until her daughter stood on the platform receiving her nursing diploma from the wife of the viceroy that she allowed herself to relax.

Cirrhosis took her almost immediately. It was as if the bacteria itself had waited for Dtui to graduate. Years of bad diet and poor living conditions took their toll on her tired body, and by her daughter's third paycheck, Manoluk was already too weak to work.

The morgue position paid only a dollar a month more than the wards, but for Dtui every dollar counted. She didn't partic-ularly like the idea at first. She'd entered nursing to keep peo-ple alive, not put them in jars. But the morgue dollar and anoth-er from overtime paperwork helped pay for the drugs that kept her ma alive.

The previous coroner had been a kind man, a pencil-thin bachelor trained in France. He helped Dtui out whenever he could, but he was helping many others on his modest salary and she didn't like to ask for more. He had escaped across the river with all the others, not knowing what punishment his sophisticated family name might bring down upon him.

The Pathet Lao takeover could have been a disaster for Manoluk, had Dtui missed any paychecks. Nobody was sure whether they'd keep their jobs in the new regime, or be paid, or be sent for re-education. Dtui and Geung went to the morgue every day as usual and mopped and dusted and whacked cockroaches, waiting for some news of their fate. But in the beginning it turned out that the new system worked in their favor. The government made a demonstrative point of helping the disadvantaged. Although money became scarcer and virtually disappeared after two drastic devaluations, Dtui was able to stock up on rice and canned supplies.

That's how things still were. Manoluk had her better and worse days. Mostly she just lay and read. Like the mysterious monk had predicted, Ma was having a better year. Her cirrhosis wasn't getting any worse, but she still needed medical attention that wasn't available in Laos. If Dtui got the posting to the Soviet Bloc, she could live dirt-cheap and send the living allowance back. It was double her salary. Girls she knew were doing just that.

She could dream of finding a wealthy man to marry and end all their suffering, but although the Lord had blessed her with intelligence and kindness, He hadn't made her slender or pretty enough, so their future was in her hands.

She sat in the dim glow of the desk lamp staring at the molds in front of her on the desk. She was wearing her Chinese overalls and a thin layer of red dust. Earlier, at the hospital garden allotment, she'd been assigned to rescue as many *gaaw* turnips as she could from the impenetrable crust of the back lots. Those that hadn't been baked by the heat had become inedible fossils.

She should have gone straight home to see how Manoluk was

doing, but instead she'd become fascinated by this case. She'd made agar casts of the teethmarks on teacher Chanmee and was comparing them with the two other sets. Whatever had savaged the teacher had also bitten deep into the throat of Auntie See. There was no doubt about it.

Although the front morgue door was open, she heard a knock on the frame outside. She called out: "Who is it?"

"Civilai."

"Come in, comrade."

Civilai walked through the dark vestibule and into the office. "Hello, Dtui. Siri not here?"

"He's not back yet."

"Ah, those Luang Prabang girls."

"He sent a message this afternoon that he's trying to get a flight. There's some problem with his paperwork."

"You surprise me."

"They say he can't get a *laissez passer* out of Luang Prabang because he didn't have one to get in. So, officially he shouldn't be there."

"Ridiculous. This was official business."

"It was, but the doc didn't come back when he was supposed to. He missed his helicopter ride. I think he upset the local governor as well."

"He never gets too old to break the rules, does he? I'm convinced if he weren't the national coroner, he'd be in prison."

Dtui sucked air through her clenched teeth.

"What is it?"

"He might end up in prison anyway."

Civilai shook his head and went to sit at the doctor's desk. "What's the old dog done now?"

"I don't know, uncle. But two uniformed policemen have been here twice looking for him. They say they have a warrant."

"What for?"

"His arrest."

"What on earth do they think he's done?"

"They wouldn't tell me."

"I'll get Phosy to look into it. We can't have our only forensic surgeon locked up. I'll see what I can do about his travel pass, too."

"Thanks, comrade."

He looked around at the office. "Hot, isn't it?"

"Damned hot."

"What's that you've got there?"

"Teeth marks."

"Aha."

He carried his chair over to her desk and looked at the clear gray molds. He poked a finger into the side.

"This looks like. . . ."

"It is."

"Very ingenious. Did you think of it?"

"I was just about to, but Siri got there first. A second case came in today with identical marks to those on the old lady. We think it's a bear."

"In Vientiane?"

"One escaped from the garden of the Lan Xang."

"Not that old dishrag? It hardly seemed alive. But I bet it had a chip on its shoulder. Now I see why Siri had me hunting for an animal expert."

"Did you find one?"

"I certainly did. He apparently knows something about bears, too."

"Good. I can't wait for Siri to get back and sort this all out."

Civilai looked at her through his thick glasses. "Well, don't then."

"Don't what?"

"Don't wait."

"You mean I . . . ?"

"Siri always says you're five times smarter than he is, not that that's so difficult. But you seem like a very able young lady. I'll

arrange the paperwork, and you can go talk to the fellow."
Dtui's smile surpassed the glow from the lamp. "If you think
you're up to it."

"You bet your red flag I am, uncle."

"Good. That's settled then."

"What do I need paperwork for?"

"You can't just waltz up and start chatting to foreigners, you
know."

"He's foreign?"

"Russian. Like the vodka."

"Oh."

The pervading atmosphere of socialist xenophobia in and
around Vientiane had added to the culture of mistrust.
Although there were very few actual spies, there were enough
imagined ones to keep everyone on their toes. The Lao didn't
dare go up to a foreigner in the street, because they didn't know
who might be watching or what they might be thinking about
the relationship.

The remaining foreign teachers or long-term residents found
themselves with fewer and fewer friends the longer they stayed.
Maids and gardeners and drivers had to report weekly to the
Department of Foreign Affairs. They reported car registration
numbers, overheard conversations, and names of suspicious visitors. It was frightening to imagine such power in the hands of
a maid.

Although the politburo was keen to accept foreign aid from
the Soviets and Vietnamese and to invite their experts to act as
advisers, they didn't actually want too much mixing with the common people. So it was that Dtui spent a sleepless night worrying
about her date with the foreign devil on the following morn.

She'd never spoken to a white man before.

Doin' the Exorcism Conga

The compact Luang Prabang Town Hall was more romantically lit than usual. They'd brought in an extra supply of beeswax lamps, as per instructions from the Department of Culture. They certainly weren't to use electricity, as the manual said it disturbed the natural harmonics. The building was draped in white threads, and candles on small clay stands burned along the perimeter walls.

If there had been any tourists, this would certainly have been a highlight of the slide show back home. Except that they wouldn't have gotten in. Siri stood in the shadows opposite and watched a bizarre parade of witch doctors arriving, as if out of various dreams, to be frisked by two tough soldiers at the gate.

Those without spiritual connections were turned away and joined the large crowd of bemused locals gathered beyond the wall. They pointed to well-known but barely-seen shamans like stars arriving at the Oscars. One wizard-like man with thick white hair down to his naked knees drew "ahh's" of admiration from the gathering. Two short round Hmong women, like zeros, came together with a stick-like man in red.

There were old ladies in white sheets wheeling barrows of artifacts, men in eyeless hoods guided by young children, animals in sacks squealing anticipation of a sacrifice, small troupes of cymbalists clattering around intoxicated mediums, and transvestites in makeup brighter than the lamps. The carnival of

freaks was interspersed with wise folks who had found shaman-
ism thrust upon them and had no desire to turn themselves into
circus performers.

Siri attached himself to the tail of the parade and flashed his
ID. Once inside, he was overwhelmed by the humidity and the
scents of the assembled witchery. Incense smoke of contradict-
ing spells tangled like clothes in a washing machine.
Excremental odors of petrified piglets and body sweat and
cheap cigarettes all wafted through the room.

The authorities had laid out folding wooden chairs in neat
rows as if this were a gathering of normal people attending a
political seminar. On the raised platform stood a table with four
seats and name place-cards. As yet, the owners of the names had
not taken their seats. They were waiting for the assembly to settle down before making an entrance.

But this was an assembly of the unsettleable. They sprawled
and faced about and ambled around, greeting old friends and
arguing old scores. They turned their chairs into walking creatures that mingled with them. And soon the raised table was a
forgotten focal point overlooking an unruly scrum. It was all
most sociable, but terribly un-socialist.

Siri was content to squat against the side wall and watch the
show, but the white-haired man caught sight of him and walked
unsteadily over. As he got closer, Siri could see there was little
more to him than hair. He was a skeleton painted pale pink.

"Yeh Ming, Yeh Ming. How would you be?" the old man
asked. He seemed truly delighted to see Siri, or whoever it was
he saw. He held out a sprig of finger-bones that Siri shook carefully. The sound of the man coming down to sit beside him was
like a wind charm being lowered to the ground. Siri was surprised that his hidden shaman was so obvious to this old man.

"You know Yeh Ming?"

"Certainly. Certainly. How could I not? You're an ancestor to
many of us."

"You know, I haven't actually met Yeh Ming myself. I only found out about him last year."

"You could do worse, boy, much worse. You see that particularly obnoxious looking woman there with the glued hair? She carries around the unsettled spirit of *Sisadtee,* who died a horrible death. She spends all her time seeking revenge on those who cut off her limbs."

"Is there any chance that I could talk to you about Yeh Ming? There are a lot of things I need to learn."

"Why not? Why not? Come by tomorrow, around the second sunrise."

"Where do I find you?"

"You know the Pak Ou caves?"

"I've heard of them."

"I'll wait for you there."

"When exactly is the second sunr—?"

His question was drowned out by the shrill blasts of two referees' whistles. The sound cut through all the chatter. The four local dignitaries had arrived at the high table and were being ignored. The men at either end had taken out their whistles to shut up the audience. Between the blowers sat Comrade Houey and his tough friend who was, according to his name card, the head of Provincial Security.

Even with all the whistling, it was still some minutes before the chairs were turned and half-turned toward the stage and the noise had abated. One of the whistlers began a well-worn introduction to his boss.

"Respected comrade brothers and sisters, the Northern Lao Administration of the Democratic Republic is honored to have you here this evening. It gives me great pleasure to introduce the holder of no fewer than twenty-eight distinguished service citations, two medals of. . . ."

He went on. Siri whispered to his partner: "Do you have any idea what this is all about?"

"Oh yes. Oh yes. But I came anyway. I wouldn't have missed this for the world."

". . . His Honor, Comrade Governor Houey." The other three men at the table applauded. The audience didn't, although one of the sacrificial cocks crowed in its sack. Houey stood and looked with arrogance around the room.

"comrade shamans," he began. "This morning, the king and queen, the crown prince, and several members of the former royal family were transported, for their own safety, to the Northeast."

There were dissatisfied murmurs from the crowd. Siri now understood where his helicopter had gone. Houey didn't pause for effect. "As you all know, since December of 1975, the man you referred to as 'king' has been a normal citizen like you or me."

"But without the respect," someone shouted.

"Who was that?" Houey asked angrily.

"Sorry," said the heckler in a softer voice. "It's one of my malevolent spirits. I can't stop his outbursts."

Comrade Houey looked sternly at the simple man who was calmly whittling a wooden doll.

"Considering the harm the royals have done to our beloved homeland over the centuries, comrade, your king can think himself very lucky that he's still alive. If this were Russia, they would all have been in the pit long ago. You tell your malevolent spirit that."

"He heard, boss."

Some of the shamans tittered, and Comrade Houey got the feeling that he was being made fun of. He wasn't a man who took abuse in any form. He had to bring these mumbo-jumbo charlatans into line. He was wearing a thick gray shirt, Lao style, outside his trousers. Through the material, he took hold of the butt of the handgun tucked into his belt. Most of the guests noticed the gesture but didn't appear to worry about it at all. Houey continued.

"Because of the influence you people have been allowed over the years, most of the general population up here is in fear of the spirits. This seriously affects their concentration when it comes to studying the doctrines of Marx and Lenin. There isn't enough room in the simple mind of the rural poor for conflicting influences. The only spiritual stimulation they need is of a political nature. One man, one doctrine."

"Which one?"

It was the same rude spirit speaking through the whittler.

"What?"

"Well, you said there can only be one politico–spiritual influence, one doctrine. But you mentioned two: Marx and Lenin. That's confusing for the brainless peasants. Which one do they choose, arsehole?"

"Guards. Take this man—"

"It's not me!" the man protested.

"—and his malevolent spirit outside."

Two men in uniform escorted the embarrassed shaman out of the room. He walked calmly, but his resident troublemaker protested and blasphemed all the way to the door and beyond it.

"Pagan commie leeches. King killers. Organ suckers!"

When he was gone, Houey took a deep breath and continued.

"I'm delighted to announce that on this historic day, marked by the long-overdue erasure of the vestiges of the illegal royal bourgeoisie, the so-called royal spirits are also to be disbanded."

There was a shocked buzz of comments around the room. Some laughed.

"Quiet! I've called you here today because you are going to summon the spirits and give them an ultimatum." The murmur became a sea of bold comments and jokes. The audience laughed at each one-liner, and order was lost. The men on the stage reached for their whistles, but a much calmer sound quieted the rabble. Siri's partner had begun to speak. His voice somehow threw a blanket of respectful silence over the others.

"If you please, Comrade Houey. It isn't that easy."

Houey looked for the source of the comment and saw the white-haired man and Siri for the first time. He became very angry.

"Is that you speaking, or are you a damned ventriloquist's dummy as well?"

The man rose silently and far more elegantly than he had sat down. It was as if he were rising to full height in an elevator.

"No, sir. It is I. I am Tik Kwunsawan. I was the official court spiritual counselor to the late king. Forgive me for speaking out of line, but requesting the spirits to attend isn't like calling pupils into a classroom. The conditions—"

"Well, Comrade Tik Kwunsawan, this is no request. If the spirits wish to be a part of the new democratic republican network, they have to toe the line. This is a State directive."

"The State may as well order a rainbow, Comrade."

"Sit yourself back down, old man. You don't have any exclusive rights on the spirit world. Look."

He held up the stapled booklet that was in front of him on the table.

"This is the official manual, issued by the Department of Culture in Vientiane, for the summoning of spirits."

No joke could have drawn a bigger laugh than that. Not even Tik, rejoining Siri on the floor, could hold back his laughter. Siri recalled his visit to the Ministry the day after the suicide. He imagined the officials in one of those bare offices poring over the texts to remove all the religious and royal references from the ceremony. He was surprised there was enough left to make a manual. But it was significant that they hadn't seen fit to ban the practice altogether. Too many of the country's remaining three million people had come through life on the wings of the spirits to banish them completely.

The whistlers brought the crowd back to order, but before Houey could continue, the glue-haired woman asked: "If you can do it all with that little book, why do you need us at all?"

"Right," echoed the audience.

Houey shook his head and smiled. "This is the very essence of socialism, my sister. We work together as a team. You help me and I help you. Despite our differences, despite our deep resentments and doubts, cooperation turns us into one single body. We are all here ultimately for one purpose."

"And what is today's purpose, Young Brother?" Tik asked in his quiet voice that still carried to the rafters of the building. Houey nodded to a sheet of paper in his colleague's hand.

"We shall be giving the spirits this ultimatum." Tik held back his smile. "They will have three choices. Three choices are very fair, I believe, considering the State has no legal obligation to them. The first—"

"Wait," Tik said. "If these are conditions for the spirits, they should be here to listen, don't you think?"

Siri looked around. It was obvious that the shamans were confused. How could they bring the spirits to a place like this? Houey consulted with his table mates. "That won't be necessary."

"How else can we be sure to get the message to all of them?" Tik asked.

"We were thinking you could sort of pass it on to them once we'd left, or when you got home." Houey seemed to be getting paler.

"Goodness me, no. Much easier if they hear it straight from the horse's mouth. Let's bring them here."

"That really isn't—"

"Brother and sister shamans," Tik said in a louder voice, slowly rising to his full height, "let us invite the spirits to attend their final meeting."

"I don't th—"

But Tik had already begun a peculiar dance. He chanted in a tongue that neither Siri nor the others present had ever heard. If anything, it bore a close resemblance to a North American Indian rain dance.

Tik moved slowly toward the throng, raising his hands to call down the spirits and stamping his feet in time with his chant. At first the shamans looked on as if senility had taken him. But then one Hmong little lady zero stood and followed him, copying his rhythm and his gestures. She chanted counterpoint to his bass.

The men on the stage looked sideways at one another, not knowing how to react or what to say. This wasn't what they had planned. One by one, the shamans stood and joined the line. One child dragged her hooded father by the hand. A toothless gash appeared on one ancient woman's face, and she leaped to her feet, twirling and yelling like a young girl.

Siri had never attended a mass séance before and he was unsure of the protocol. But there was one point of which he had no doubt: there wasn't a hope in heaven or hell that this fiasco would bring any spirits into the Luang Prabang Town Hall. He laughed to himself, got to his feet, and joined the conga.

The rhythm was strong now, and all the guests were riding the giant eel around the room. Those with instruments played them. Those without screamed and whooped and looked upward to the invisible heavenly ropes, down which the imaginary ghosts would descend. Without warning, Tik stopped and turned his head so suddenly toward the top table that the four men held on to their heartbeats. The room shushed.

"They're coming," Tik said in a whisper. He looked up, reached his hands to the ceiling and seemed to swell up. "Welcome." All the others followed suit. Some twitched, as if the fit of the arriving spirits didn't match their bodies. Some gulped them in like air. Some took handfuls of them and forced them into their ears.

And, like a sudden audience of zombies, Tik and the shamans turned toward the stage as slowly as melting ice, as silent as the graves from which the spirits had supposedly come. With eyes large and unblinking, they stared at Houey with their teeth bared.

The cadres on the stage were apparently in some kind of trance too. They looked down on the sea of drooling, staring people possessed by god knew how many angry spirits. It was a situation the manifesto hadn't prepared them for. The crotch of the Security Officer's trousers was already a noticeably darker green than the rest of his uniform. Siri could just see the parchment-white face of Comrade Houey. He had to give the governor credit: he didn't run. In fact, although his voice trembled, he attempted to continue his speech.

"comrade spirits. It . . . it has been vested in me, as a . . . a representative of—" He'd forgotten to breathe and the words stopped. He smuggled in one or two deep breaths to calm himself. "As a representative of the LPRP, to make the following announcement."

He held out his hand to the head of Security for the document. But the man had turned into some kind of granite bust. Only his eyes moved, scanning back and forth across the faces of the shamans. So Houey wrenched the paper from his hand and read. His own hands shook so badly that it was amazing he could catch up with the typed words.

"You shall be given three . . . and this wasn't my idea. You shall be given three alternatives."

He looked up for a response but received none.

"Firstly, you may go to the Northeast to join the ex-royals."

A thought occurred to him.

"Of course, you'll have to make your own arrangements for . . . well, your own arrangements."

He was going to add "for transportation," but thought better of it.

"Secondly, if you intend to stay in Luang Prabang, you will have to work in the service of the temples. A specific. . . ."

He noticed that some of the shamans had started to vibrate, not unlike spin-dryers. It unnerved him.

"A specific temple will be assigned to you, and you will be

ordained as temple spirits. Naturally, you'll have to share the workload."

The vibrations increased, and one of the whistle-blowers began to back away across the stage.

"Thirdly, if you select neither one nor two, you will be. . . ."

He looked up, wondering if he dared read on. The vibrations were more pronounced, as if the audience was one large jelly. He took another breath. The second whistler was on his way out.

"You will be banished from Laos. Naturally we don't want to resort to that, so it's better you take the other alternatives. I suggest you all go away and think about this. I won't expect your decision right away. We're all fair here. Is that clear?"

Silence. The Security chief's chair crashed to the floor as he ran for all he was worth to the back door. Houey stood alone and vulnerable.

"Good. Th . . . then that concludes our business for th . . . this evening. So I. . . ."

Foregoing the usual farewell speech, Houey turned, walked at first, then jogged to the exit. The sheet with its three conditions wafted like a leaf, back and forth, down to the wooden stage.

There was a polite pause to give the officials time to get away from the building. But when all was clear, Tik turned, smiled, and nodded to the crowd. The shamans fell into a fit of mirth and merriment unseen in Luang Prabang since the days of the old regime.

Farewell the Beer Smuggler

Ounheuan and his wife had decided on an early night. They had to get up early the next morning to smuggle whiskey and beer from across the river. They weren't criminals, of course. Most shop owners had to engage in a little rowing in order to have something to sell.

In spite of their good intentions, they hadn't been able to get a wink of sleep. First, there were the howls. Then there came one almighty dog fight. Now, one of the creatures, obviously injured, was growling and whining in front of Ounheuan's shop. His wife decided she had tossed and turned enough.

"Oun. Can't you go down and do something about that?" There was no reply. She thumped him on the shoulder, and he grunted as if barely roused from a deep sleep. "Come on, lizard shit. I know you aren't asleep. It's annoying you as much as it is me."

He continued a well-practiced snore, and she knew the worm had no intention of going down to the street.

"Bum."

She yanked back her side of the net and got to her feet. Tightening her sleeping cloth above her fleshy breasts, she walked to the window and looked down. A wooden awning jutted out between her and the door of the shop. Although she could hear the wounded dog, she could see nothing in the unlit street.

"Shit."

There was nothing humane about her going downstairs. She wasn't about to apply first aid to the bleeding paw of some street dog. Those mongrels would have off your hand as soon as look at you. Probably give you rabies too.

No, the plan was to grab a long stick and prod the creature far enough away that she could get some sleep. She found the perfect thing: a length of lead piping. If the poor thing were too injured to limp away, she could whack it over the head and put it out of its misery.

The padlock was on the inside of two large metal doors that concertina'd together to fill the frontage of their open-terraced store. Still grumbling, she took the key from the glass cabinet and unfastened the lock. The sound of the rusty door scraping along the ground was the last thing Mr. Ounheuan remembered before his pretend sleep became a real one.

When he awoke, the sky was already cobalt blue and he knew

they'd overslept. The sun would soon be up and their dealer on the Thai side would take his booze elsewhere. He cursed his stupid wife and turned toward her place on the mattress, but she wasn't there.

Perhaps she'd gone by herself. Didn't want to disturb her sleeping loved one. Some blasted hope. He went down to the shop, scratching his crotch through his football shorts.

"Phimpon, what the hell are you playing at?"

The metal door was open and the key poked invitingly from the padlock. "Oh, right. Let's just leave the place wide open so anyone can help themselves to—"

He'd reached the doorway and froze there, hardly believing what he saw. Two black crows flapped but stood their ground. The gravel front of his shop was alive with the squirming bodies of cockroaches. There were thousands of the little buggers feasting on some sticky substance he couldn't make out in the halflight. He assumed it was some sort of treacle.

But then he recognized the remains. Two, perhaps three dogs had been ripped apart. He picked up a length of lead pipe that lay in the doorway and went at the crows that were feeding on them. They retreated the length of the pipe, but still didn't fly away from their dream breakfast.

It was then, beneath their flapping wings, that Ounheuan noticed something that turned his stomach. He could barely breathe. He sank to his knees and vomited. He couldn't bring himself to look again. But even though his eyes were clenched shut, he could still see the image of the hand. His wife's wedding ring on the middle finger glinted in the rising sunlight.

That Old Dead Feeling

It was no dream. Siri was unequivocally dead—in Nirvana, he hoped. Even if points were lost for being a communist, he trusted he'd earned enough to be in heaven rather than the other place. He saw no fire, heard no pop music, and smelled no opium smoke, so his hopes were high.

"Have you forgiven me, Lord?"

It was the trunk that confused him.

He'd arrived back at the temple long after midnight. When he left the Town Hall, the celebrations were still raging. No guards had stayed around to lock up.

It was the most fun Siri could remember having for a very long time. The impromptu show: the shamans impersonating the officials, the heated debate the spirits may have had as to which option to choose, the transportation problems in getting them to the Northeast. It was sparklingly brilliant entertainment for a town whose heart had been removed. But his assumption that no spirits had been awakened and summoned by the phony séance was a mistaken one.

At That Luang temple, the night guard was asleep beside the staircase. Siri walked to the prayer hall and retrieved his small bag from behind the Buddha images. He dug through the contents, retrieved his waistcloth, stripped, and went out to the earthen jars to bathe.

He was on his way back when the disturbance began in his ears. At first he assumed it was water lodged there, and he shook his head to free it. But the pressure turned to a sound. It was an annoying single note, metallic, at a pitch that set his teeth on edge. He looked around the yard to see where a machine could be to make such a row.

The temple dogs slept at peace. The birds roosted in the tree branches, all undisturbed by the jarring sound. It was evidently exclusively his. He followed it to its source, the destroyed stupa inside the blue wall. The closer he got, the more deafening the sound became, the more painful the pressure on his eardrums. He looked into the foundation of the stupa base lit by a generous moon but saw nothing. Yet instinctively he knew there had to be something in there inviting him to come closer.

He climbed over into the square of bricks and picked his way carefully to the center. There he cleared a place to kneel and began to dig with his hands. Beneath the rubble, the earth was soft, mulched, teeming with the warm bodies of earthworms. The deeper he dug, the louder became the sound.

He was so focused on his task, he didn't notice what was happening around him. The destroyed stupa was slowly reforming. The bricks were reattaching, the mortar hardening. But Siri had only one thing on his mind: to stop the awful sound.

Although he couldn't yet see it, his hand arrived upon the source of his discomfort. As soon as he took hold of the cool stone, he knew what had lured him there. He could feel the leather thong attached to its loop at the top of the black amulet. He knew the shape and the slight ripples of its indentations. He could feel the power of *Phibob* that now had a hold of him. It was pulling him—pulling with the strength of a thousand malevolent spirits—pulling him with the conviction of righteous revenge—to his death.

He felt his arm being wrenched downward through the soft earth writhing with the bodies of maggots and centipedes. They attached themselves to his naked skin and helped to drag him down. He couldn't let go of the amulet even when his shoulder was flush with the ground. Like a man about to vanish under water, he looked up to take a last gulp of air.

That's when he saw that the stupa was complete and he was entombed. The air was musty with the exhalations of four hundred years. That was the last taste on his final breath. That lungful didn't last him long once he was buried and traveling on down through the earth. He held it for as many seconds as he could, but he knew it was futile. He was packed in dirt. There was no point in trying to breathe again. All he could do was wait.

As a coroner he knew the process well. His face twitched as the muscles went into spasm. The death rattle rose in his throat, and he allowed himself one last agonized struggle until his heart stopped beating. Just before the machinery shut down completely, the metallic drone stopped and he heard his name called. It was a beautiful sound. Hearing is the most stubborn of the senses and the last one to leave a dying person.

He was aware that his pupils were dilating, and he could feel the warmth seep from his body. In another hour he would be stiff with rigor mortis. There was no more movement, just the calm that comes from sensing the cells and tissues dying at their own sweet pace, a process that could take weeks to complete. His goosebumped skin would be the last to submit to death.

In less time than it takes for a fish to fry, the nerves feeding the cortex of his brain would be gone and whatever feeling remained would come as an observer hovering outside the packet he'd once lived in. By then, it would be as useless as one of the plastic bags that floated down the Mekhong.

He looked up into the golden light that showered onto him, and through the beams he saw the smile of the Lord. He sighed and smiled back at his maker. It was a relief, after all. He felt no bitterness. He'd had enough of life. He wasn't depressed, just bored. It was as if he'd read the book of living and knew how it ended. There was nothing more to learn. He abandoned the body and reached out to Buddha.

That's when the Great Plan proved to have a page or two missing. The Lord's head shook from side to side as if he didn't want Siri after all. His face distorted and out of it grew a trunk. It snaked down to where the soul of Siri hovered and blasted the dead doctor with a torrent of warm breath that stank of stale peanuts.

The Randy Russian

Dtui, reflecting the bright sunlight from her crispy white uniform, stood at the gates of Silver City. This was neither a city nor silver. It was a walled-off compound two minutes' walk from the new Monument to the Unknown Soldier. It was reputedly from here that the KGB did its spying. Some said it was the Soviet Union's response in Southeast Asia to the American spy factory in Bangkok. But very few people had actually been inside to report on what other evils it contained.

Ironically, before they were turfed out, the American Secret Service had operated from this same compound. Some people speculated that "silver" referred to the glint of sunlight from the refined opium on its way to the troops in 'Nam.

Dtui scanned the tall green gate and the walls to either side, but saw no sign of a bell. The paint was dusty, so she kicked at the metal. It sounded much louder than she'd intended. There were a few silent moments before she heard a soft "Who is it, and what do you want?"

"I'm Nurse Chundee Vongheuan."

Such was the name with which she had been christened, although it didn't get a lot of use. At birth, it was customary in Laos to give your children ugly nicknames to ward off baby-hungry spirits. There were Pigs and Prawns and Camels and no end of Dtuis—Fatties. Many Dtuis grew up to be slim and beautiful, but Chundee Vongheuan lived up to her name. "I'm here to see Mr. Ivanic. I have an appointment."

A small square spyhole opened near the top of the gate, and a man looked down at her. He was either very tall or standing on a chair. She held up her paperwork from Civilai.

"Okay."

One flap of the gate was unlocked and held ajar, barely wide enough for her to squeeze through the gap. A second guard stood inside with a brand-new AK47. The stock was still in its plastic wrapping. Guard One wasn't tall. He had a stepladder.

Dtui found herself between two sets of gates, like a security air-lock. Before they could let her through the second gate, they had to lock the first and follow certain procedures. The small guard reached out as if to frisk the big nurse, but she took a step back.

"Think again."

"I have to search you."

"Over my dead body. Look in the bag if you like."

He did look in the bag and found the agar molds.

"What are these?"

"Top secret."

"Oh. Okay."

There was a pause.

"Hot, isn't it?"

"Damned hot."

With that, they unlocked the second gate and prodded her into the compound. It was a sprawling area with lovely old jujube trees and a mishmash of buildings that made the place look like an open-air museum of bad architecture. She'd expected one of the guards to follow her in, but the gate was re-bolted behind her and she was alone.

She walked to the nearest building, a two-story wood-and-brick affair that was neither a house nor an office. She stood in the open doorway and called out: "Sorry. Is somebody here?"

There was the sound of scurrying, as if some animal had been disturbed, then silence. "Hello?"

A good-looking young man in rolled-up shirtsleeves, slacks, and bare feet came from one of the rooms wiping his hands. He stopped suddenly at the sight of the white-clad nurse before him.

"Eh?"

"Good health."

Over the man's shoulder she saw a girl in a military uniform emerge from the same doorway and head off in the opposite direction.

"My name's Chundee Vongheuan. I have an—"

"—appointment to see Mr. Ivanic. Yes, I was expecting you. They didn't tell me you were a nurse." He shook her hand and smiled. "I'm Phot. I'll be translating for you."

He slipped his feet into leather sandals in the doorway, and they walked across the compound. Dtui felt somewhat unnerved to be so close to this young man who must have had women falling at his feet. He wore his good looks like a comfortable old jacket.

"What do you all do here?" she asked.

"Oh. Absolutely top secret. Can't possibly tell you."

"All right."

"But these two buildings are Lao secret police."

She laughed.

"They spend most of their time planning ways to infiltrate the insurgency groups and bug foreign embassies. That little warehouse is 'weapons training.' Soviets and Lao with a dozen words in common learning how to arm and disarm bombs. Most of us give the place a wide berth."

"I get the idea you aren't secret police."

"Hell, no. I was doing engineering in Moscow. The bastards dragged me out with a year to go on my degree so I could come here and help them make sense of their Soviet allies. They say if I give them three years, they'll have their own people back from Russia and I can go finish my Master's."

They walked to the far end of the compound, and a small troupe of stocky Lao women in sequined tops and tights walked between the buildings.

"My God, why are they walking around in their underwear?"

"That's their uniform. This is the performing arts end of the yard. Those girls are training to be acrobats. Lao girls are self-conscious about wearing tights and leotards, so the Russians make them dress like this all day till they get used to it. The Soviets have been here for six months, training them in circus skills. There are all types: jugglers, trampolinists, trapeze artists."

"What's wrong with Lao performing arts?"

Before he could answer, a deep roar diverted their attention. As they rounded the gymnasium, they came face to face with a black puma at the end of a long leash. It was only three bounds and a leap from the man at the other end of the rope. He was in his fifties and wore impressive thigh-high boots. Dtui doubted he could see those boots himself, as his stomach bloated out in front of him like an enormous ball of cheese. His darkly handsome eyes peered from a nest of curly red hair that wove into a wild crimson beard.

In his left hand he held a short whip, a seemingly ineffective weapon against such a potentially dangerous creature. But the beautiful black animal prowled obediently to an overturned oil drum and climbed onto it. There she sat and reared upward, clawing her fists through the warm air.

A small class of young men, most of them weighing not half of the creature they were watching, sat cross-legged in the shade of an egg yolk tree.

"That's your Mr. Ivanic," Phot told her. "This is what he does for a living."

Ivanic cracked the whip lightly. The animal stepped slowly to the ground and stood looking at the students like a diner perusing a menu. Ivanic walked toward the back of the gym where cages were lined up beneath a canopy of coconut leaves. He tugged gently at the puma's leash, and she started to follow him.

This was a duty she'd performed daily for several weeks without much thought. But on this day something got into her. Whether it was crankiness from the breezeless heat, or boredom at the unchanging diet, it's hard to say. It was as if it just occurred to her that a rope didn't work in both directions. There was nothing restraining her from the big man's back.

She quickened her pace so the rope sagged, then broke into a loping run. The students gasped but were too shocked to call out. The puma was already at the base of her leap, coiling into a spring, split seconds from her prey. Dtui screamed.

Then suddenly without turning or changing his pace, Ivanic cracked the whip underarm and behind him. The very tip of the leather snapped against the animal's snout. She shook her head angrily and stumbled over her bent front legs, turning a complete somersault and landing a foot from where the Russian now stood.

She was more humiliated than injured. The students clapped in appreciation, but Ivanic called something out to them. One of the other interpreters standing behind them translated his words.

"Mr. Ivanic reminds you how important it is to let your animal know that you're always awake, always alert, and that you have eyes in your arse."

The students laughed and clapped again and Ivanic led the humbled animal to its cage. It entered with no further fuss. Dtui and Phot walked over to it. There were four mesh cages the size of rattan ball courts. The puma's neighbors were a small Lao wildcat and a very old lion whose ribs protruded like some ancient xylophone. The fourth cage was shrouded completely in long, worn stage curtains. There were other animals, untethered elephants, deer, and buffalo that wandered around the courtyard in pairs, as if in search of an ark.

Phot spoke to Ivanic, who seemed delighted to see him. They joked about something; then, with a big smile, the Russian reached out one dinner plate of a hand to Dtui and gave her the once-over with his eyes. She shook his hand but avoided the stare.

"Mr. Ivanic is always happy to see a big woman in a uniform," Phot translated.

Although her mother had warned her that all Western men were lecherous dogs, the greeting caught her off guard. For once in her life, she didn't have a cutting response. "I'm glad Mr. Ivanic has time to see me."

With the Russian's hand uncomfortably against the small of her back, they all walked into the little gym. There they sat around a small card table at one end. At the other, young women were sending their limbs in directions Dtui could never have imagined sending hers. One young lass stood on one leg and held the other against her cheek, the toes pointing to the ceiling. Ivanic noticed Dtui's grimace.

"Mr. Ivanic asked whether you can do that."

"Yes, easy. As long as the leg wasn't attached to me any more."

The Russian laughed with his whole body and went to give her a hug. She avoided it by bending down to her bag. She dug out the concrete cast and laid it on the table.

"Could Mr. Ivanic tell me what animal produced these marks?"

Ivanic took up the concrete mold and spread his huge hand over it. He looked up at Dtui, not smiling now.

"Mr. Ivanic wonders where you got this print."

"It was from my boss's garden."

"So there isn't a connection between this and the killings of the women?"

"You know about that?"

"Remember where you are, Nurse Chundee."

"Right. Secret Police, I forgot. No, this one wasn't connected to the killings."

"Mr. Ivanic believes this is the print of a Malay black bear. He estimates it to be quite large for its breed."

"Did he ever see the bear at the Lan Xang?"

The response was quite heated.

"Mr. Ivanic is very angry at the treatment that bear received. He's delighted the animal escaped."

"Is this print likely to have been made by that bear?"

"It's very likely."

"Does he believe that bear could have killed two people?"

The response was long and seemingly complicated. Phot had to ask for clarification of a number of points. Dtui's eyes wandered again to the poor deformed girls and the knots they were tying themselves into.

"Mr. Ivanic is most concerned that there is a 'shoot to kill' order out on the bear. He has tried without success to convince the director here to rescind the order."

"Why?"

"According to him, there's no way an Asiatic bear could do the damage we've heard about."

"But they are carnivorous."

"Yes, but they're the most passive of the carnivores. They may eat small slow animals or kill something wounded and eat that, but it's very unlikely they'd attack a large animal. It's unthinkable that they might attack and kill man."

"Even if they'd been tortured by man?"

Phot asked the question and smiled at the answer.

"Revenge is a trait exclusive to us humans. Animals don't get even. They can be very forgiving."

"Is it totally impossible?"

"It's so unlikely, it's hardly worth thinking about."

Dtui took out the two agar molds and put them on the table. Mr. Ivanic clapped his hands and said something to make Phot laugh.

"Mr. Ivanic says if he'd known we were having a party, he would have brought something to drink."

"Well, you keep him away from these jellies. They were set on the skin of dead people."

"These are the marks from the bodies?"

"Yes."

Phot explained and Ivanic looked very seriously at them. Again he held his huge hands over the marks to judge the size. Then he shook his head.

"Are they bear teeth?"

"No."

"How can he be so sure?"

"Mathematics."

"Mathematics?"

"Mr. Ivanic says bears have forty-two teeth. Whatever bit into the flesh of these unfortunate women had fewer. Even if all the teeth didn't leave a mark, there still isn't enough space from the back teeth to the front. His guess is around thirty."

"And what would that make it?"

"Mr. Ivanic says it was a cat."

"I take it he isn't talking about a lap cat."

"He's referring to a very large cat." Ivanic said something, stood, and walked toward the door. "We should follow."

In front of the cage where the defeated puma now lay, Ivanic formed his hand into the shape of a jaw and opened his fingers toward the animal. It responded with a relatively subdued growl and gave Dtui a view of its awesome teeth.

"Wow. What was your puma doing on the night of the ninth?" she asked through Phot. The Russian laughed and squeezed her shoulder.

"Mr. Ivanic said she was with him all night, officer. But the cat you're looking for is even bigger than this one."

"How much bigger?"

"Perhaps a tiger."

"He thinks there's a tiger on the loose in Vientiane?"

"He agrees it doesn't sound very likely."

"Could he be wrong about the number of teeth?"

The men got into a discussion. "Even if he were wrong about the numbers, and I doubt he is, the set of the mouth is different. Cats' teeth are shaped for cutting. The bear's are adapted for grinding. Your mold shows teeth that could only have been for cutting. In fact, Mr. Ivanic can't recall ever seeing such sharp teeth. It was as if. . . ."

A deep drowsy growl came from the covered cage. Dtui looked up and didn't notice the exchange of glances between the trainer and the interpreter.

"What's in there?"

"It's just another animal."

"What type?"

"It's a panda."

"Why's the cage covered?"

"Mr. Ivanic says the animal has just recently arrived from China and it's reacting badly to the heat, as we all are. In such circumstances, pandas are known to regress and become nocturnal until they can acclimatize."

"So it sleeps in the day and gets rowdy at night?"

"Something like that."

"But it's a bear?"

"Yes."

"Do you think I could take a look at its teeth? I just want to try to understand the differences Mr. Ivanic has described for myself."

"It's sleeping."

"Maybe it sleeps with its mouth open. I do."

A discussion ensued between the men, and it was clear that they disagreed on the decision. Mr. Ivanic seemed to think it was all right as long as they didn't wake the creature. The Russian untied the edge of the curtain, took Dtui by the hand and led her into the flap between the drape and the bars of the cage. The thick material did a good job of keeping out the sun. The only light oozed up from the points where the curtains didn't quite reach the ground.

She could barely make out the slow breathing shape at the rear of the cage. Its face was away from her. All she could see were the contrasting black and white markings and the piles of uneaten fruit. She would have stayed longer till her eyes became accustomed to the dark, but she was suddenly aware that Mr. Ivanic's hand was moving from her back slowly south. It was time to get out.

Phot was waiting for them, smoking a cigarette.

"See anything?"

"Not much. It was too dark. I thought pandas were bigger than that."

"It will be. He's still quite young. Nurse Chundee. . . ."

"Call me Dtui."

"Dtui, if you don't mind, it would be better if not too many people knew about our panda. It hasn't exactly cleared customs."

"Illegal alien?"

"It came in on a transporter overnight from Kun Ming. The paperwork would have taken weeks. The thing would have starved to death in Customs if we'd done it officially. You understand?"

"My lips are sealed."

He interpreted their conversation.

"Mr. Ivanic thanks you for your cooperation. He would like to show his gratitude by inviting you for lunch at his private rooms."

"I'm sure he would. But I'm afraid that although Mr. Ivanic is marvelous with animals, he doesn't have nice manners when it comes to Lao women."

"You want me to translate that?"

"Absolutely."

"Good for you."

Second Sunrise

The second sunrise came at around 8 A.M. It was when the first sun had risen high enough to reflect from the golden dome of Xiang Thong temple. For many in Luang Prabang, this marked the time to head for work—which, in turn, explained why so many people stayed in bed on cloudy days.

Siri sat on the white steps in front of Pak Ou cave. It was a pocket in the face of the cliff that overlooked the confluence of the Mekong and the Nam Xuang rivers. Its most remarkable characteristic was what it contained: there were thousands upon thousands of Buddha images of all shapes and sizes. The coroner had been up to look at this unguarded population that dated back hundreds of years. He wondered how long it would be before some disreputable pirate rowed in under the cover of darkness to fill orders for Thai antique shops.

He wondered from which direction his shaman friend would be coming. As far as he'd seen, the cave wasn't deep. It ended at a rock face. That's probably why he was startled to hear Tik's voice behind and above him.

"What are you doing down there, Yeh Ming?"

"I'm waiting for you. How did you get up there, Brother?"

"I live here."

"Then I can't think how I missed you, unless I mistook you for a Buddha."

Siri climbed back up the steps. The old guru wore nothing

more than a small cloth knotted around his organ and its appendages. Siri shook a hand that clicked like knitting needles, and the two men went into the cave. The doctor nodded toward the images. "I was thinking of a curse to protect these gentlemen."

"You're several hundred years too late, boy. These are better protected than the national treasury."

"How? Anyone can walk off with them."

He was being led slowly into the shadows at the rear of the cave.

"Walk off, yes, and many have been walked off with over the years. But believe me, not one thief has lived a happy life as a result of it. I can't tell you how gruesome are the fates that await he who harbors a Pak Ou Buddha. And through the marvelous sense of direction they possess, these statuettes will all gradually find their way back here where they belong."

They reached a rock wall that Siri had inspected earlier. It appeared sheer and unbroken, but Tik walked confidently toward it at an angle and exposed the optical illusion. It was as if he were being swallowed by a solid rock. Siri approached it more carefully, and it wasn't until he was almost nose-first into the wall that the gap showed itself.

He followed close on the bare heels of the old man. They walked along a tunnel lit by scattering fireflies until they arrived at a small cavern, which was illuminated from above. Somehow, natural light filtered down through crevices in the rock, even though they must have been deep into the mountain.

The hollow was littered with scavenged refuse; cans and bottles, flotsam from the river, piles of rescued royal street signs, cloths of various hues and patterns, bleached animal bones, and piles of indescribable rubbish, all meticulously cleaned.

Tik scooped a half coconut on the end of a stick into a pool and handed the water to Siri, who took a sip. It was curiously effervescent, quite delicious as water went. It gave him a slight thrill and he decided not to drink too much of it. He hadn't come looking for excitement.

Tik sat cross-legged on the floor and stared at his guest. He was a man who didn't waste time creeping up on the point. "I feel you should be dead."

Siri joined him on the ground. "How could you know?"

"How could I not? How could I miss the incredible force you drag behind you? A powerful shaman and a wild pack of angry spirits could hardly arrive in Luang Prabang without my knowing. Tell me. Begin with this morning."

Siri related the events leading up to his death: the sound, the stupa closing around him, and the feeling of being dragged below the earth. He told him how he knew beyond a whisper of a doubt that he was dead. Tik gave an admiring chuckle.

"Ahh. They're devious, the *Phibob*. Those from the south especially so. Yeh Ming has obviously made some powerful enemies over the past thousand years."

In two hands he took up a large square tin with the words HUNTLY AND PALMER BISCUITS printed on the front and slowly began to circle it clockwise in front of him. Something inside seemed to be rolling around.

"Then you don't think this is just revenge for my helping the soldiers cutting the forest in Khamuan?" Siri asked.

"Goodness me, no. Yeh Ming has been exorcising malevolent spirits for many centuries. He has a sizeable opposition in the spirit world."

"And this morning was an attempt to get even?"

"It's a little more complicated than that."

The tin was rotating faster, and Tik muttered an incantation under his breath before turning it upside down on the earth floor. He pulled it away like a child hoping to see a completed sandcastle. Instead, Siri noticed a broken egg, some small bones, and a slither of animal entrails. Tik studied them.

"In a way, Yeh Ming is in his twilight era. Perhaps that's why he's chosen such an unimpressive host."

"Thank you."

"He has been dormant for a while, am I right?"

"Apart from the dreams, I didn't know he existed until last year."

"And recently, certain abilities have awoken in you?"

"Yes."

"That is what has alerted the *Phibob*. You should never have taken him back to Khamuan. There were too many memories there, too much hostile spirit activity. The *Phibob* have the scent now. It's like the wildcat who senses that the deer is wounded. They won't settle until they have destroyed Yeh Ming's final temple."

"Where's that?"

"Not where, *who*. You are the temple in which he has chosen to end his centuries."

"Oh shit. Why?"

Tik looked up from the reading.

"What do you know of your father?"

"Not a damned thing."

"Your birth father was Lao Heu, a renowned Hmong shaman and a direct descendent of Yeh Ming. Before you, he had hosted the soul. Between them, they put together a . . . how can I put it? They put together a retirement plan, and you were it."

Siri's mind was spinning. After seventy-two years, he suddenly had a father and a history. He wasn't sure he really wanted to know. Ignorance had served him well enough all those years.

"I don't. . . ."

"As soon as you were born, a ceremony was held to make Yeh Ming your guardian spirit. Naturally, that put you in a very dangerous situation. They sent you away from your home so you wouldn't suspect you had a connection with the spirit world. Not knowing and not pursuing witchcraft was the insurance policy that kept you and Yeh Ming safe.

"The life of the soul is cyclical. If left to its own devices, it would never end. You would have carried it, then it would have passed on to another. But Yeh Ming had caused something unheard of in the world beyond. He had created an enemy of the *Phibob* that over the years became powerful in its own right.

"It was dangerous and needed to be destroyed. As it was created out of revenge for Yeh Ming, the only way to stop the *Phibob* was to end the reign of your guardian. It was hoped you would go through your life as a simple man, never calling on the great shaman to perform. It was hoped you would achieve a non-violent death and allow Yeh Ming to crumble peacefully with his temple."

"How do you know all this?"

"The details I see here in the bones and the entrails, but the story is already folklore."

"I'm a legend?"

"Don't be conceited. It is Yeh Ming who is the legend."

"How did I cheat death this morning?"

"Good fortune—or, more accurately, good karma. The *Phibob* cannot inflict direct harm. No one is physically struck down by an evil spirit. But they are able to get into your mind. There are many unexplained deaths, usually of men in their sleep without plausible cause. This is the mischief of the malevolent spirits.

"The *Phibob* can convince a sleeping person he has died. This morning they dragged your mind below the earth, confined you inside a stupa. It was so real, so convincing that your subconscious was certain you could no longer breathe. Once your mind has lost that battle, there is no point in your body continuing to function. It shuts down in defeat. Dastardly clever."

"So, how . . . ?"

Tik used a chicken bone to draw a line of yolk from the egg to the intestines.

"You had performed a selfless act earlier in the day."

Siri thought back.

"The elephant?"

"Its soul wished to repay your kindness. The spirit of the

elephant is a thing of marvel. The Lord Buddha said 'Of all footprints, that of the elephant is supreme.'"

"It kept me breathing?"

"It reminded you to start again. That and the golden Buddha beneath which you slept. I doubt the Elephant God could have saved you alone."

"I was actually dead. I know it."

"Welcome back. You appear to have a second sunrise."

"What can I do to keep the *Phibob* from doing me in again?"

"That's more complicated. To do their damage, they need a trigger. Is there something that symbolizes them to you?"

"Yes."

"Tell me."

"A black amulet. They used it to get to me. It was destroyed in Khamuan, then re-emerged in Vientiane, whole."

"It certainly wasn't the same one."

"It was."

"Oh, in your mind it may have been. But if you had asked someone else to describe what they saw, it would not have been a black amulet."

Siri's thoughts raced back to the day of the date, to Lah and to the gift. Was it possible she'd given him something else? Was the amulet in the box a mirage the *Phibob* had put there? He felt foolish.

"And you saw it again here?" Tik asked.

"I felt it. It was buried in the destroyed stupa. I didn't actually see it, but I knew it was there."

"Then that is the portal through which the *Phibob* can enter your soul."

"What can I do?"

"At the source there is usually a reverse image. It could be a mantra or an object that negates the effects of the black amulet."

"There is. They gave me a white talisman in Khamuan."

"Show me."

"I don't carry it."

"You're foolish. It must be with you always. Where is it?"

"In Vientiane. In my house."

"Then I suggest you get there as soon as you can. I don't value your chances of cheating death twice. Remember this: if you die a natural death, Yeh Ming can rest in peace; if you suffer a violent unnatural death, he will be cursed to eternal hell amongst the evil spirits. You must avoid the latter at all costs."

"Right. I'll see what I can do."

The Man of His Dreams

It was while he was searching for Mr. Inthanet's house on Kitsalat, while simultaneously endeavoring to avoid a violent and unnatural death, that Siri ran into the man from his dream. It was so unusual for living people to appear in his dreams that his natural first assumption was that this was a dead person walking along the main street.

It was the footman who'd served the king beneath the fig tree and exploded messily after introducing the helicopter pilots. He had the same straggly chin beard and hair that hung like a hula skirt around a bald dome. If anything, he looked more Ceylonese than Chinese and, to Siri's professional eye, very much alive.

Without putting too much thought into why, he changed direction and followed the man at a distance. He had a confident Western swing to his gait, and his clothes suggested that some thought had gone into their selection. His large stomach was accentuated by the tonic sheen of his traditional Lao shirt. It was as if he wore such clothes through choice, not obligation.

The man crossed the street and walked along the short drive into the Hotel Phousy. Through the glass door, Siri saw him take a newspaper from the stand at reception, exchange a few friendly words with the clerk, and walk through another door into the dining room. This told Siri one or two things.

A man would only eat in a sophisticated hotel if he were a guest or comparatively wealthy. As the newspaper was Lao, he wasn't a foreign tourist. And the cut of his clothes announced that he wasn't a waiter or cook.

Siri pushed open the double doors and walked into the small lobby. The receptionist was a middle-aged man whose spectacles only had a lens on the left side. The right was open to the elements.

"Good day, comrade," he said, suspicious of this bagless visitor.

"Good health. I was just passing and I thought I saw someone I once knew come in here: a dark man with a beard and a stomach."

"That would be Mr. Kumron?"

"Kumron—that's right. I haven't seen him for such a long time, I wasn't sure it was him. He's put on weight. What's he doing these days?"

"You can go and ask him yourself. He's in the restaurant."

"Oh, I don't want to trouble him. I doubt he'd remember me. But my sister would probably be interested to hear how he got on. They once had a . . . relationship."

"I see. Well, she'd be pleased to hear he's done very nicely for himself, very nicely indeed."

"Oh, good."

"In fact, until recently, he was an adviser and confidant to . . ." he lowered his voice ". . . the Royal Family."

"You don't say?"

"I do. He and the king were like this." He crossed his fingers in front of his nose.

"Goodness."

It was then that the clerk seemed to suddenly remember some advice he'd once been given about not trusting strangers. Although it may not have been exactly memorized, he did have a speech at hand for such an occasion.

"The Royal Family has been sucking the blood from the

country and its people for centuries. It's a relief that we're now free of the tyrant and can work together to rebuild our great land."

It was an uninspired rendition.

"So, old Kumron's probably on his way to re-education too, if he was part of that blood-sucking."

"Ah, no, comrade. Mr. Kumron is a very intelligent human being. The party has found a way to use his expertise to further its advances in the northern region."

"The Party gave him a job?"

"He's running several large projects, I believe."

It all became crystal-clear: the king's adviser, the attempted rescue, the removal of the Royal Family, and the payoff. The pilots had said it: "We were betrayed."

For what other reason would a living man appear in his dream, if not that he had died in some other way? Siri was no fan of royalty; he wasn't even that fond of communism; but he was a man of principle. He believed that whatever creed a man chose, he was dependent on the trust and honor of the men and women who followed the same creed. In Siri's mind, a betrayal of that trust was sinful.

He'd survived his forty-odd years of jungle warfare not only because of his ability to fight when necessary or run when necessary—any animal could do that; he'd survived because of the people around him. Their lives were interconnected. You had to know that a comrade was good to his word and would sooner give up his own life than sacrifice yours. That's how it had been in the early days, anyway.

Kumron had achieved the exalted position of adviser to the king. He had earned a place in the old man's soul. But in order to save his own status, he'd given up information about the escape attempt. He had ended the Royal Family's last hope of survival. With so few true friends left, this betrayal would have been a final poisonous arrow in the *kwun* of the Royals. The man shouldn't have been rewarded. If honor meant anything in this day and age, he should have been executed. But did anyone know?

Siri realized that he was still at the counter and the clerk was staring through his single lens, waiting for the next question. He also realized that he was the only one in a position to do anything.

"You know?" Siri said. "Perhaps I will go and say hello after all."

He walked through to the brown wood and red vinyl dining room. Its air was being conditioned by a large grumbling machine along the back wall. The small tables were unlaid, apart from one. There Kumron sat with his back to the door reading the newspaper. In front of him was a sight rarer in Laos than a two-headed naga serpent—a cool bottle of beer.

Siri knew that what little success this attack might have depended on how cleanly Kumron believed he had gotten away with his betrayal and how guilty he felt about it. The doctor walked around the table and cast a shadow on the newspaper. When Kumron realized he wasn't the waiter, he looked up.

"Do you believe in ghosts, Comrade Kumron?"

Kumron was a calm, dignified man who seemed unflustered by this question from a stranger. He smiled politely. "Perhaps I could ask the name of the person asking the question."

"In the long run, my name won't make any difference. I'm just a messenger."

The waiter in a short-sleeved once-white shirt and kipper tie assumed Siri was joining Kumron and dragged over a second chair.

"Please," the waiter said, but Siri didn't sit. The boy retired to the kitchen doorway.

"On the evening of the tenth, I spent his last night with a mutual friend at an orchard in Pak Xang."

"I see. Then won't you join me?"

There was something slightly less authoritative about his voice.

"No. We talked of a number of things. He surprised me at

how forgiving he was when it came to the dealings of the PL. He held no animosity toward the local cadres here who had thrown him out of his palace. There was only—"

"Sir, if this is a private conversation I think it would be better conducted elsewhere. Would you like to join me in a beer?"

He no longer looked at Siri's green eyes, which had burned uncomfortably into his own.

"No. I'm nearly finished."

And here came the lie Siri hoped might destroy the destroyer.

"He said there was only one person he could never find it in his heart to forgive."

Although his expression remained passive, Kumron's face drained of color like whiskey poured from a bottle.

"You betrayed him."

"I don't know who you are, sir, or why you came to me."

His voice trembled. The suddenness of the accusation had overwhelmed him. He'd had no time to compose himself. It was as if the king were standing before him, exposing his treachery.

"You thought you were too clever to be found out, Comrade Kumron. You thought he would never suspect you, his most trusted confidant. He believed you were a friend. I'm disgusted with you, as was the whole family."

"I . . ."

Kumron could put up no fight because he was certain he had been undone. Siri walked around the table and leaned into his ear.

"The reason I asked you about ghosts, Comrade Kumron, is because I believe the remnants of the Royal spirits will ruin you sooner or later. I'm sure you know of their power."

And his pièce de résistance, "Prince Phetsarath and I will see to that."

And he left.

He had been about to add "We both have thirty-three teeth," but as yet he wasn't sure he did, and he decided enough damage had been done. Through the dining room window he could see the man crumpled in his seat, no longer the successful dignitary. This old man would now have to haul the twin burdens of guilt and revenge. Siri decided that a small battle for loyalty had been won and he dedicated the victory to his gardening friend. He didn't know whether the king knew of Kumron's role in his downfall, but it didn't actually matter. A good lie in the right place can make up for any number of wrongs.

Dtui had been sitting for an hour in front of the office of the politburo member. She hadn't made an appointment with Civilai. That wasn't a particularly Lao thing to do. Appointments were rarely kept. She knew he had to come to his office eventually, and much sooner than she'd expected she was proven right. He walked along the corridor, flanked by two officious men who seemed much more flustered than their boss ever had.

"Nurse Dtui," he said. "You brighten my day with your smile."

"Comrade Civilai, can I have a quick word?"

The two aides protested.

"Why, certainly. I'm informed someone else is on his way to see me, but you're most certainly my priority."

In his office, Dtui told him about the talk with Ivanic.

"So," she concluded, "do you think we can call off the 'shoot to kill' order on the bear? It's been worrying me sick."

"Dtui, my darling, remember where you are. It's incredibly hard to get the simplest things done here. But it's next to impossible to get anything undone. By the time the order's filtered down to the bozos with the guns, it'll certainly be too late."

"Can we change it to a tiger hunt?"

Civilai laughed. Despite the difficult life he'd lived, he remained a jocular man who was intelligent enough to take his status and circumstances without too much seriousness. He had the presence of mind to greet all his disasters with a Lao laugh. This attitude worried many of the more somber Party members.

Some wondered if he was really interested but, in fact, he cared deeply about most things.

"The Department of Interior already thinks I've got a few screws loose. If I start announcing open season on all varieties of wild animals roaming the city, they'll have me in a straitjacket. Don't forget, this is all on the say-so of a Soviet circus performer."

He could see that the matter was starting to depress her.

"Don't you worry. Our army sharpshooters are all terrible shots. They'll probably miss."

"I know this all looks really silly, but our office is responsible for fingering that bear. I wouldn't be able to sleep a wink if I thought she got herself shot on our recommendation."

"When's your boss coming back?"

"I'm off to meet him at Wattay now. He got a regular flight, I guess, thanks to you."

"It's who you know. Is this a new morgue service, going to meet Siri at the airport? Or do you just miss him?"

"He called. He wants me to go and take care of a guest. He's bringing someone, but he wouldn't say who."

"Whatever next?"

There was a knock at the door and one of the aides poked in his head.

"He's here, comrade."

"All right."

Civilai escorted Dtui from the room. In the waiting area a round-faced Chinese-looking man with a paper fan sat on a bench between two others sweating in suits. His curly hair sat on top of his head as if he were balancing a bunch of black grapes there. He was out of shape and wore a tight safari suit that proved it.

Civilai went over to him and shook his hand. He looked up through his unfashionable glasses but didn't bother to stand.

"Comrade Kim, how nice to see you again," said Civilai without enthusiasm.

It was translated by one of the damp shirts, but there was no verbal reply, just a nod. Civilai dragged Dtui up beside him.

"This is Nurse Dtui. She's a soldier in the revolution to cure the sick, toiling day and night to look after our small but blossoming proletariat and make them well enough to further the cause of the blah, blah, blah, etcetera, etcetera. You know the lines," he said to his Korean-speaking aide. The man had recently returned from Pyong Yang.

"Just keep the bull going till I get back."

He smiled at the visitor and walked Dtui to the door.

"Who was that?"

"Secretary of the North Korean Workers' Party. Next president. Son of present President Kim, a.k.a. 'Living God.' I'm supposed to keep the bundle of joy entertained while he's in town."

"You don't sound very enthusiastic."

"Really? If you knew what cultural delights the boy finds entertaining, you wouldn't be enthusiastic either."

"I tell you one thing, uncle."

"What's that?"

"He wouldn't get a date if he wasn't the son of a Living God."

At Wattay in the late afternoon, the Antonov 12 bounced along the runway until it came to a skidding halt. The previous year, in one of the major policy decisions of the Transport Department, perhaps the only one, Air Lao had become Lao Aviation. But the only investment that entailed was a few pots of paint. Bits still fell off during turbulence and on the few days it was working, passengers still vanished in a fog of air-conditioning.

The plane purred with achievement some eighty meters from the arrival shed so the passengers would have to plod across the sticky tarmac with their bags. As per Siri's confusing instruction, Dtui had commandeered a *songtaew* taxi and told the driver to wait with her. She saw her boss come down the wobbly airplane steps from the rear door. He waited at the bottom until a sprightly old man with cropped white hair joined him. They walked quickly toward the shed, engaged in a serious conversation.

Siri gave a pleased smile and waved when he saw his assistant perspiring in the uncooled arrival lounge. She was behind a short barrier that separated the arrivers from the waiters. This was a domestic flight, but there were two officers in a booth checking every passenger's *laissez passer*.

Siri was escorting an illegal traveler bereft of paperwork, so this could have been the start of a bureaucratic nightmare. But as he'd assumed, it turned out to be quite simple. The officers only checked the papers of those who crowded around them waving their travel documents and their house registrations and their birth certificates and their lists of signatures. One could avoid this melee by not going to the booth at all.

Siri and his friend skirted around the riot and walked past the man on the barrier with the confidence of travelers whose documentation was in order. It helped to be met by a nurse in uniform and a driver. You had to be someone for such a reception.

"Dtui, this is Mr. Inthanet. He's—"

Before Siri could complete the introduction, two policemen in non-matching uniforms strode up to the group. One of them held a small passport-sized photograph. Dtui recognized the men.

"Dr. Siri Paiboun?" one policeman asked, although he apparently knew already.

"Yes."

"You are under arrest, comrade. Please come with us."

Everyone but Siri seemed surprised.

"May I ask you what the charges are?"

"They'll tell you at the police station, Doctor."

The other policeman took Siri's arm lightly and gestured for him to head outside with them. The prisoner looked back at the amazed faces of Inthanet, Dtui, and the *songtaew* driver. He held up four fingers to his traveling companion and winked.

"Don't panic," he said, smiling. "Please take Mr. Inthanet to my house and make him comfortable. I'll be there shortly."

But the last they saw of Siri that day was the back of his head in the police truck being driven out of the airport carpark. Dtui looked at the mysterious visitor, smiled, shrugged her shoulders, and said:

"Hot, isn't it?"

"Damned hot," he replied.

"So, how do you know Dr. Siri?"

A Land Without Lawyers

On the Saturday morning, the three observers watched the condemned man eat three hearty breakfasts. There were metal bars between Siri and his friends. Dtui, Phosy, and Civilai watched him chewing happily on glutinous rice, and raw fish in a sauce spicy enough to self-combust. None of them spoke because they were still too dumbfounded.

It was Phosy who first learned of the heinous crime Siri was accused of. He called Civilai and told him. Dtui only found out about it when she turned up at the jail. She couldn't believe her ears. They were all too shocked to discuss it. So they merely watched Siri eat the breakfasts each of them had brought for him.

"Aren't you going to say anything?" Siri asked at last looking up from his food. "It is hard to eat in front of a committee. . . . Hot, isn't it?"

Still there was silence. Even though the door to the cell was open and the guard had gone for coffee, the guests had preferred to sit outside. This made Siri feel like one of the animal exhibits at the Lan Xang Hotel. Eventually, Civilai gave in. He shook his head and said "Siri, you're the national coroner."

"That's not my fault. I didn't ask to be."

Civilai found this response to be amazingly flippant, even for Siri.

"Fault or no fault, you are it. You represent the Party. Whatever entered your head to do such a thing?"

Siri wiped chili sauce from his chin.

"Now there you go. What happened to 'innocent until proven guilty'? Thank goodness I'm not being judged by a jury of my peers. You'd all see me to the gallows."

"Then tell us you didn't do it."

"I'm not making any statements until my lawyer gets here."

"You haven't got a lawyer. In fact, I doubt whether there are any left in Laos. They're damned fine swimmers, I hear."

"What about you? You studied law."

"I'm not representing you. I think you're as guilty as Nixon himself."

Dtui couldn't hold back a little laugh. Siri didn't notice.

"It shouldn't make any difference what you believe," he said. "You just have to convince them."

"Siri, in two hours you have to go up in front of Haeng. You may recall that you haven't exactly endeared yourself to the judge over the past six months. In fact, it could be said that you've crawled under his skin at every opportunity. And you have to defend yourself against charges that could very well result in your incarceration on Don Thao for the remainder of your sorry life. Personally, I think it's time you started to take this seriously."

"Hear, hear," Dtui agreed.

Siri put out the spice fires burning in his chest with a swig of Dtui's home-squeezed juice.

"Ah, Dtui. Your mom squeezes a grand guava."

"Siri!"

"Relax, brother. They won't get me. Even if they try, all I have to do is point them in the direction of January 1976."

"And what's that?"

"That's the day your revolutionary council set a match to all the books. And one of those books happened to have the national constitution written in it. And once that had gone up in smoke, all the laws went up with it. Remember?"

Phosy felt obliged to enlighten the good doctor. He was a policeman, after all, and he knew about abuse of the system only too well.

"comrade, let's for a second forget about laws. Let's imagine instead that you've pissed off the people that run the country. Let's suppose that they can make up a fitting punishment off the top of their heads. What if they decide that letting you off will be a signal to all the other citizens to do anything they like and get away with it? Not having laws goes in their favor. They can do what they like with you."

"You're still all assuming I'm guilty."

"I'm not," Dtui said faithfully.

"Thank you."

Trials were a rarity in the Lao People's Democratic Republic in those days. The hearing of Siri's case was closed to the public to avoid hysteria. In fact, beyond the police and the Department of Justice, nobody knew about it. Not much negative publicity for Party members made it into the *Siang Pasason* newspaper.

As this was merely a hearing, it was conducted in the Justice canteen. The tables had been rearranged to give it the feeling of a real courtroom. Judge Haeng, in a nice pink shirt with collar buttons, sat at the front table by himself.

Young Mr. Sounieng, arguing for the State, sat at another table with the chief witness to Haeng's left. Siri, arguing for himself, had his own table to the right. The small official group of onlookers sat on chairs facing them all. Civilai and Phosy were amongst them.

The accuser, and the insistent pursuer of action on the matter, was Siri's silent neighbor, Soth, the crooked official from Oudom Xay. He glared across at the accused with a half toothpick protruding from his snarling gray teeth.

Credit had to be given to Judge Haeng. He was certainly out of his depth, still having presided over nothing more taxing than divorces and domestic disputes. But he had all the formal language down and he kept order quite nicely.

Everything sank or floated on the evidence of the only witness. Haeng called him to describe in his own words what he'd seen on the night of the ninth. Soth was obviously a man who considered the outcome of the trial a formality.

"It was about four of the morning," he said. "I'm a light sleeper, so when I heard the sound it woke me up straight off. I forgot where I was for a minute and thought someone was chopping down trees in the forest. Then I remembered we was in the suburbs. So I grabbed me handgun and walked out into the—"

"Did anyone else hear this supposed sound?" Siri interrupted.

"He can't ask me questions," Soth protested.

"In fact he can," said Haeng. "Dr. Siri is representing himself at this hearing, so he has a right to cross-examine."

"Good on you, son," Siri mumbled.

The man glared at them both.

"Don't seem fair, if he's the accused."

"Just answer," Haeng said. "We'd all appreciate it."

"I sleep at the front. Me wife and the kids sleep at the back."

"So in fact they didn't hear?" the judge asked.

"Doubt it. I didn't ask them. But I certainly did. I went out to the lane and looked up the end of it. And I see him standin'—"

"For the court's benefit, would you be kind enough to give us a name? For the records."

Actually this wasn't a trial and there wasn't a stenographer, so there were no records, but the judge certainly had a handle on the proceedings.

"Him. Dr. Siri Paiboun," said the man. "He was standing down the end of the lane with a machete, and he was chopping away at the pole what holds up the government speaker."

"The radio speaker?"

"That's it."

"So, what did you do?"

"Do?"

"Yes. You had a gun. Did you try to stop him?"

"Yeah, of course. Well, no, not exactly stop him. It was too late. He'd cut a sizeable bite out of the pole, so when I went out it was already swaying back and forward. The wire was stretching till it was the only thing holding the pole up. Then it snapped and the whole lot come crashing down. The speaker got smashed to bits. It was total vandalistic desecration of government property; an act of treason against the great LPRP."

"So then what did you do?"

"Went back to bed. Nothing you can do at four in the morning. I reported it the next day, but the perpetrator had already fled the city in panic."

"Thank you."

Judge Haeng tapped his pencil loudly on the desk in front of him as he chewed over the facts. It annoyed everybody in the canteen. He finally looked up at Siri.

"Dr. Siri, these are indeed serious charges. Do you have anything to say?" Siri stood. "Doctor, this is a hearing, you don't have to stand up."

"I prefer to. If I may, I'd like to ask the witness one or two further questions."

"Go ahead."

"Now, sir. You say this dream you—"

"Dr. Siri!"

"Sorry, your honor . . . this scene you witnessed was at four A.M."

"You know it was."

"Just yes or no will do."

"Yes," Soth snarled.

"Well, as far as I can recall, the area around the radio post is overhung with large trees. On the ninth the moon was already quite full."

"If you say so."

"Then the trees must have cast quite a shadow. It would have been very difficult to identify a person standing there."

"There's nothing wrong with my eyes. I saw what I saw."

"Just yes or no."

"I saw you."

"Even though the pole is . . . was fifty meters from your front gate?"

"I saw you."

"I'm sure you saw something, sir. But you must agree that everything comes down to your eyesight."

"It's perfect."

"Really? It wasn't so perfect last night, was it?"

Civilai and Phosy exchanged a low-eyebrow glance. Judge Haeng stared quizzically at Siri.

"You think not?" the man said mockingly. "Well, it was good enough to see you. You think I didn't see you?"

"You tell me."

"I saw you all right, and I brought the evidence here. You think this kind of thing's going to scare someone like me?"

He reached into his shoulder bag hooked over the back of the chair. Mr. Sounieng, the prosecutor, obviously wasn't expecting any evidence. He shrugged toward the judge. Soth produced a small wooden image. It was porcupined with pins like a West Indian voudou doll.

"See, Judge?"

He held it up so that Haeng and the observers could get a good look at it.

"If this isn't harassment of a key witness in a treason trial, I don't know what is. He crept up and hung it off me front porch early this morning. I saw him."

Haeng called for one of the guards to bring him the doll, even though he could have just reached out and got it himself. When it arrived, he studied it. It bore not the slightest resemblance to the witness.

"And you saw Dr. Siri hang it there this morning?"

"As clear as I see you, Your Honor."

Of course, that was the end of the hearing. Siri was given back his belongings and allowed to go home. If the case hinged on the eyewitness, and the eye of the witness saw a man on his front porch who was actually under lock and key in the Sethathirat police station at the time, that had to be the end of the case. Even if one were convinced Siri had wielded the machete as most of the observers were, one would have to admit it was a thoroughly effective technicality. Even the witness was struck silent by its blow.

When Dtui—on her lunch break—arrived at the canteen, it was all over. Phosy filled her in with the details, and they had a cup of iced Chinese tea to toast the doctor's survival.

"Of course, they'll put up another pole," Phosy said.

"Probably, but at least he'll get a couple of weeks of peace."

"I'm guessing he didn't think it'd cause such a stink. He probably assumed the neighbors would be delighted and nobody'd report it."

"I'm sure this has taught him a lesson. You have to love him, though, don't you?"

"Certainly do."

They sipped at their tea with smiles on their faces.

"Hot, isn't it?"

"Damned hot."

"Phosy?"

"What, Dtui?"

"Can I ask you something about the bear chase?"

"All right."

"I know we convinced you that the killings were done by the bear."

"Yes."

"Well, I don't think it's the bear any more."

"You think there's something else running round biting big chunks out of people?"

"It's all very odd. According to an expert, the marks aren't from a bear's teeth. They're more likely to be from. . . ."

"Go on."

"A tiger."

Phosy spat out the mouthful of tea he'd just taken and coughed a laugh to follow it.

"Really? So we now have a bear and a tiger and goodness knows how many other wild animals all running around Vientiane, and nobody's seen any of them? What? Are they in disguise?"

"Right. It's ridiculous, I know. But something's killing people and if it isn't the bear, what I want to know is what or who could be doing all this damage. If nobody's seen an animal, it has to be a person. Phosy, I want to go to the islands on Nam Ngum Reservoir."

"Whatever for?"

"Every convicted, known, or suspected murderer is locked up there. If it isn't an animal doing these things, I want to know who could be capable of it."

"There are two things you're forgetting, Nurse Dtui."

"What?"

"One, I'm a policeman, and you—and I'm not denigrating your calling—are a lab nurse. I investigate crimes. You look at pimples under a microscope. That's the way of the world. If anyone were to go to Don Thao Jail, it would be me."

"Great. When you going?"

"Second, if your killer were in Don Thao Jail, he'd be in Don Thao Jail. Anyone who got over the wall, got past the trigger-happy guards, and avoided the mines would doubtless drown on the swim to the mainland. And then there's the teeth. Wouldn't he have to have a mouth the size of a wok to keep those teeth in? What about that little problem?"

"I just look at pimples. You're the investigator. That's for you to work out. So?"

"So?"

"Are you going? If you don't, I will."

Phosy blew out an exasperated breath.

"I tell you what. I'll save us both a trip. There's a man we can go and see right here in Vientiane who probably knows the crazies on the islands better than they know themselves."

"Groovy. Let's go."

"Not so fast. He won't be around till this evening. Anyway, shouldn't you be at the morgue?"

"No problem. My boss just escaped a firing squad. I don't think he'll be coming in to work today."

"When he does, I for one want to know how he pulled that Siri double trick."

"Oh, I think I know the answer to that."

The Toad Impersonator

Inspector Phosy decided enough was enough. He'd given the doctor plenty of time to solve the mystery of the royal chest that still sat unopened at the Department of Culture. Siri had asked for a few days, but had said nothing upon his return other than "Be patient, Phosy. Be patient."

Well, his patience was used up.

He went by the hospital to see Constable Nui, who was now sitting up in bed and talking but could remember nothing of the day he had tumbled down four flights of stairs. Neither could he recall the women gathered around his bed, nor the face of the person now asking him questions. His memory slate had been effectively wiped clean.

Phosy rode the lilac Vespa the few blocks to Nam Poo fountain and looked up at the ministry building, black and ominous against the purple sky. He felt the adrenaline pumping and was annoyed he'd let the talk of curses get to him. Like on all Vientiane nights, there was hardly any noise and precious little light. He took a clunky Russian flashlight from his pack and climbed down from the bike.

As the top two floors of the building were officially his crime scene, he was in possession of keys for the main door and the access door to the sixth and seventh levels. There was never an armed guard on duty in front of the building, as the authorities still believed they were in control of crime and insurgency in the capital. At ten, an elderly watchman would arrive from his fishing duties and camp down on the ground floor. It was a small and futile attempt to discourage trespassers.

Phosy was about to cross the road when he heard a rustle from the bushes that circled the waterless fountain behind him. He turned sharply and shone his flashlight there. He didn't say "I know somebody's in there" or "Come out with your hands up," because the shudder in his voice would have given away his fear. Instead he ran the beam along the crispy brown leaves and saw nothing. He heard something, though. It was the burp of a toad. He lowered the light and thought to himself: "So now you're afraid of frogs. If you jump a mile at every lizard and rat and moth, Officer, you might not even make it to the seventh floor."

He turned his back on the embarrassment and started to walk across the road. This time he ignored the leaves that rustled behind him and the continued burping. In the near distance, he could see the spotlight of a Thai surveillance helicopter skirting the far bank of the Mekhong. The river was a block away, the only natural water to be had in that dry city in March. The fountain had spouted nothing but Morning Glory blossoms for a year. "So why . . . ?"

The question of why a toad would be so far from water should probably have come to him sooner. It wouldn't be answered. There were more urgent questions: What was it running barefoot behind him? How did it get so close without his noticing?

Before he could turn, the strong arms had hold of him. Before he fell, he recognized the distinctive scent.

At about the same time, Siri was in his office at the morgue. He'd neglected his duties for too many days. One corpse had come and gone, collected in pieces by her distraught husband who wanted to know why there had been no autopsy.

To avoid the loud glare of the fluorescents, he read Dtui's reports by candlelight. She was very precise and neat, and she'd doubled the size of her letters so Siri could read everything. He laughed at her account of the visit to Silver City and her description of the fat Soviet with a head like uncooked noodles. She was wasted on morgue reports.

He read of her suspicions on the similarities between the two previous attacks and the killing of Mrs. Ounheuan. He was certain his nurse would make a very fine coroner, but it was unlikely to happen. The Health Ministry would never consider sending a nurse on one of the valuable Soviet scholarships. She had a certificate that was a long way short of a medical degree, and, rightly or wrongly, Party members appeared to get most of the plum placements. She was bright, but it would take her over a year just to make head or tail of the Eastern European textbooks.

He was about to reach into the drawer to take out the three sets of tooth prints when, in the flicker of the candle flame, he saw the same old woman sitting at Geung's desk. She startled him at first. Chewing on her betel nut, red saliva dribbled like blood down her chin. He was no longer afraid of the spirits but could still get a jolt when they appeared suddenly. This old lady had been showing up unannounced in the office for months. In all that time, she'd done nothing but chew.

"If you want help," he said calmly, "you'll have to give me some sort of sign."

But she did nothing. He didn't recognize her from his dissection table. He'd never met her alive. She wore a Lao *phasin* and a white halter blouse. This gave him no clues as to from whence she came. Women in the country had been wearing this style for centuries.

"All right, my love. You just make yourself at home. I've got some work to do here. Yell out if you need anything."

He smiled, and to his surprise she smiled back. It was a gory smile, showing some five teeth stained black from the betel nut addiction. More bloody saliva dribbled, and she was gone.

"'Bye, then."

Before going home, Siri stopped off to see Constable Nui, who seemed convinced that the doctor was his father, long departed. His tearful wife sat on the bed beside him.

"He's been doing that all day, Doctor. He thinks I'm his dog."

Siri examined him briefly.

"I wouldn't worry," he said. "I suspect it's just concussion, and if that's the case it'll slowly wear off as his mind puts the bits back together. His reflexes are fine. That's a good sign. It takes time."

"That's what Inspector Phosy said."

"He was here?"

"A bit earlier, Doctor. He tried to get some sense out of Nui about the job he was doing at the Ministry when he had his accident."

"Well, as long as he doesn't go there himself."

"But that's just what he planned to do, sir. He said he was off to get something to eat to build up his strength to open some box."

"My God, no."

Siri was out of his room faster than a man approaching his seventy-third birthday had a right to move. Nui's wife and her sisters looked at each other in disbelief.

Nui looked up.

"'Bye, Dad." He then looked angrily at his wife. "And you. What have I told you about not getting up on the bed?"

Dtui had waited long enough. She wasn't the kind of girl to be standing around on a dark corner in the middle of the night. Her appointment with Phosy had been for nine. It was now nine-forty, and even by Lao standards that was long enough to wait.

She asked the neighbors for directions and found her way to the pretty house that had a feel of the old regime about it. She creaked open the tall wooden gate and walked into the dirt yard. An overly friendly little dog came up to her and took an immediate fancy to her ankles. She trod carefully so as not to crush the fellow and called out as she neared the house: "Sorry. Is anyone home?"

There was a light inside.

"We're home," came a woman's voice. "Come on in."

Dtui had the feeling this lady was used to visitors dropping in at all hours. She got as far as the unlocked door, and still nobody had come to meet her. She knocked and eased the door open.

"Excuse me."

"Welcome."

A middle-aged couple sat on either side of the mat, on which a simple meal was spread out. They looked up and smiled.

"Have you eaten yet?"

"Already, thanks," she lied.

"Come. Just have a little bit to keep us company."

This was the way Dtui remembered neighbors being. Even the poorest family would invite you to eat the last few scraps with them. This couple didn't know who she was. She hoped socialism wouldn't destroy all this.

"I'm sorry to arrive like this," she said, sitting at the mat on the loose parquet floor. "My name's Chundee Vongheuan, but people call me Dtui. I'm a nurse at Mahosot."

"Good health, Dtui," said the wife as she pushed the small plates of vegetables and fish to within her reach. She removed the lid from the sticky rice container and put it near the other food. The man spoke for the first time. He and his wife had interchangeable masculine and feminine qualities about their faces.

"I assume you know I'm Dr. Vansana. This is my wife, Sam."

Dtui nodded and smiled and helped herself to a small pinch of rice from the wedge.

"Good health to you both." She dipped the rice into one of

the sauces and popped it into her mouth. Sam went off to the back room.

"I work in the morgue," Dtui said, breaking off more rice. "I work with Dr. Siri Paiboun."

"Yes, I've heard of him. Most of his practice was in the jungle, I believe."

"That's him. I've come to ask for a little help on one of the cases we're working on; a recent spate of killings."

"The bear?"

There really were so few secrets in Vientiane.

"Yes. Except I'm starting to believe it wasn't the bear at all."

"Is that so?"

"Dr. Vansana, you're the visiting physician for the internment islands on Nam Ngum Reservoir?"

"That's right. For over a year."

"You must have come to know the inmates quite well by now."

"Those that want to be known, yes."

"Can you think of anyone there who might be capable of killing women violently? Any psychopathic murderers escaped lately?"

"Ahh, Dtui. People don't escape from Don Thao. Virtually the only way to get off is in a bag with your name written on a tag. There are some psychotics there, and a number of murderers. But the really serious violent criminals all seem to have been . . . removed from the general population."

"Removed? Do you mean executed?"

"I'm not even sure I should be discussing this. I'm really in no position to make such a claim."

"But it's possible?"

"I suppose."

"And the ones they kill, do they do it on the island?"

"I haven't said they do such a thing and I haven't seen it happen. But the conditions there are barbaric. People die all the time of malaria, dysentery, and the like. The facilities are quite basic, and I don't have enough medicines to treat even the most treatable illnesses. I go twice a week, and there's a new pile of bodies every time I get there. I don't have time to look at the cadavers, but I do hear rumors."

"What kind?"

"Just comments like 'You won't have to check so-and-so's lungs this week, Doc. He won't be using them no more. He upset the warden last week.'"

"That's terrible. Surely you've reported this to someone?"

"It's in the weekly report I submit to the Health Department. They pass it on to Corrections. But I doubt if anyone reads them. Conditions haven't improved at all, and I've been pushing for better sanitation and mosquito coils since I started. I just go there and do what I can. It isn't much."

Sam returned with some newly cubed papaya on a plate. She put it on the mat in front of the guest.

"Thank you."

"Straight from the tree. I hope it's ripe enough."

She joined them on the floor and watched Dtui try the fruit.

"M'mm. It's lovely. I wish we still had trees. My mom misses the fresh fruit."

"There you are. I must be psychic. I've cut down a couple more for you to take home with you. They're out back."

Dtui thanked her and ate some more of the fruit before continuing her questioning.

"Dr. Vansana, how did you get this job? It sounds simply awful."

"I suppose it's my reward for not escaping to Thailand," he laughed. "They probably think anyone with a degree who stuck around has to be a spy."

"Why did you stick around?"

"We're Lao, Dtui. We love our country. You don't help a place you love by running away when times get tough. Sam's a teacher. I'm a doctor. We didn't choose these professions because we thought it would make our lives more comfortable. I'm quite sure you didn't either."

"No. But I wasn't expecting it to be this difficult. Do you still feel like you're contributing? All you see are patients dying because you haven't got the resources to help."

"I don't kill all of them. There are those that I can help. Some get better. I focus on them."

"But none get off the island."

"I didn't say that. I said none escape. There are those that are judged to no longer be a threat to society. Some of the addicts survive. Some of the petty criminals repent."

"And they let them go?"

"It costs money to feed them all."

"Don't you think the really clever con-men get through the net, pretend to play the game just to get their backsides off the island?"

"I dare say some do."

"Do any crazies get off?"

"Not the type of crazy you're looking for."

"What types?"

"Some people with mild retardation, some memory disorders, some with delusional conditions, some—"

"Any of these delusion victims released recently?"

"Dtui, these aren't dangerous people."

"Give me an example."

"There are a few. There was an elderly lady who thought she was sixteen. She was flirting with all the male guards. Then, last week there was a young man called Seua. He's probably the most placid man you could meet. He's a big chap but calm as a catfish. He was very popular there. He was polite and helpful, so they decided to let him go."

"What was he in for?"

"Like a lot of them, it was just a petty crime. He stole food because he was hungry. He just had the misfortune to steal it from a shop that belonged to an army officer."

"What type of food?"

"Pardon?"

"What food did he take?"

"If I remember correctly, it was meat from a butcher's stall."

"And what was his delusion?"

"Dtui, this isn't the man you're looking for. I knew him and liked him very much. His disorder hadn't reached the stage of schizophrenia. I think I can recognize latent violence."

"What did he believe, Doctor?"

He looked at his wife, then at Dtui.

"He believed he was the host to an evil spirit. He always talked of it very matter-of-factly, as if he were talking about a loose tooth or a tattoo."

"Did he say what spirit?"

"Yes, it was a weretiger."

"Wait. He believed he hosted the spirit of a man who turned into a tiger?"

"No. The myth is that the weretiger is a tiger who from time to time can transform into the shape of a man. But Seua never showed any aggressive tendencies. It was all talk. Dtui?"

She was on her feet.

"Do you know what time the Corrections Department opens in the morning, Doctor?"

Then the Moon Went Out

Crazy Rajid's eyebrow had stopped bleeding at last. It had spouted enough blood to fill the Nam Poo fountain by itself. Phosy had never seen anyone who found his own blood so hilarious. He laughed so hard Phosy had no choice but to laugh with him. Perhaps, Phosy wondered, this is the letting of the mad blood. Perhaps, at the end of it, Crazy Rajid will be as sane as the next man. They could discuss worldly issues as equals. But there was no sign of it.

He wrapped a makeshift bandage around Rajid's head which seemed to simultaneously stop the bleeding and turn him into a Sikh. He dropped the Indian at the hospital, left a few *kip* with the reception nurse, and confirmed that the split would need some seven stitches. It wasn't till a patient behind him let out a startled scream that he realized his back was drenched with blood.

When the crazy Indian had first grabbed him, their heads had clashed and then the bleeding began. They'd fallen to the ground with Phosy unable to shake off his attacker. At that stage, he'd still been fearing for his life until he smelled the odor of the unwashed and heard the familiar giggle. That's when he knew it was no attack. It was a gesture of friendship; a joke, if you like. Who could tell? When you befriend a man whose mind lives on a distant star, you deserve whatever you get.

By the time Phosy had persuaded his friend to get the hell off, he was already soaked in blood. They sat together on the lip of the fountain, Phosy binding the wound, Rajid going through his impressive repertoire of amphibian impersonations.

Phosy stopped off at the station to change his shirt. There were four or five policemen there who listened spellbound to his story of how he'd fought off the giant grizzly. Then he told the true story and they booted him out.

It was an hour after the first attempt that he arrived at the Ministry to give it another go. As he parked his scooter, he looked up at the seventh floor. It seemed to glow like the elements in a toaster. He took four paces to his right and looked again. The light was gone. This was the penultimate night of the full moon. It hung large in the cloudless sky. From certain angles, it reflected from the glass windows of the building. It was time to be sensible, but he didn't retrace those four steps and look again.

His master key unlocked the main door and he stepped inside. His footsteps echoed around the empty foyer. The windows were all shuttered down there. The beam from his flashlight was so straight and slim, it only illuminated what was directly in its path. All else around him was charcoal black. He picked out the teak steps and went toward them.

There came a creak from above that he rapidly assumed had to be the old floorboards stretching out after a day of work. He hurried upward. After the first flight, the steps were coconut wood and they, too, groaned under each step.

He browsed, but didn't stop, at the first three levels. The moonlight through the odd unshuttered window cast long clawing shadows that unnerved him. But at the fourth floor he was drawn by a sound. It was faint, yet he could tell it had nothing to do with the natural aches and pains of an old building. It was melodic.

He strafed his light across the large central area and shone it into the doorway of each office. All were ajar but one. He walked toward it. The closer he got, the more clearly he heard the sound. It was definitely traditional music. If it were not for the hour, he would have assumed a careless employee had forgotten to turn off her radio. But national broadcasts stopped at nine and, given the current state of animosity, he couldn't imagine the Thais entertaining their neighbors with Lao country music.

He stood at the door and instinctively reached for a gun he didn't have. Under a recent directive, inspectors had to apply for weapons from the armory on an "as needed" basis. A total of nine signatures was called for. Uniformed officers still carried guns, but they had to get thirteen signatures if they wanted to put bullets in them. Their weapons were for show. God help them if there was a spontaneous firefight: there were guns everywhere in this country fresh from civil war.

Anyway, what good was a gun against music? He continued to annoy himself with his lack of control. He took a deep breath and threw open the door. His flashlight picked out a desk, a chair, and a cabinet: not a musician in sight. But the refrain was plainly there, hanging in the air. He walked around the desk in search of its source and came to an insulated pipe that ran from the ceiling to the ground. Perhaps in the time of the French it had carried water to the top floors, but the insulation had frayed and at one point the metal had rusted away completely. It left a large gaping hole from which leaked the sounds of a Lao harp, a xylophone, and a pipe.

As the lower floors were silent, he knew the music had to be coming from above. He had a nasty feeling that he knew from which floor. Siri's warning rang in his ears along with the wooden sounds of the instruments, but this, like it or not, was his duty. He had to lead the men through example. If he didn't arrive at the station the next day with the contents of the chest, they'd know he was as chicken as the rest of them.

He arrived at the fifth floor just as the moon went out. Where that one huge gray cloud had come from on such a clear night, he couldn't begin to explain. But he could imagine, and tonight his imagination was by far his worst enemy. The blackness dropped on him like a burned crème caramel, and all his willpower went into keeping the flashlight steady.

His hand trembled as he unlocked the door that would lead him to the top two floors. The tape across the frame was still stuck securely and confirmed that nobody had gone up since the second "accident." But as soon as he opened the door, that same mournful dirge oozed down the stairwell to greet him.

He took a step back.

"All right. There's music. So what? Pull yourself together and stop talking to yourself. There's nothing threatening about music, and there's likely a very logical reason for it."

But rack his brain as he did, that reason didn't come to him. Slowly and deliberately he followed the quivering beam up the stairs to the seventh floor. The discordant strains filled the darkness around him, growing louder and more forceful. He could almost feel the vibrations of the hammers against the wooden tiles of the xylophone.

At the top door he put his hand on the knob and it seemed to shimmer.

"Phosy, you're a policeman," he reminded himself and wished to the devil he'd taken the time to collect those nine signatures. "You are not afraid."

Voices. He heard them clear as anything beyond the door, deep mumbled male voices beneath the music.

"Go back down, Phosy. Go get support. Bring back a unit of men. And tell them what? You heard music? They'd laugh at you. Stop talking to yourself."

There was only one way to go. He squeezed the doorknob, took one more deep breath, and strode into the room.

Crockery shards crunched beneath his feet, and a scream came from all around him that was no human sound. Although his flashlight was clearly still on, it illuminated nothing. He held

it up to his face. The bulb burned brightly but it no longer shed
the type of light that could reflect. It had been disarmed.

"What . . . ?"

In the otherwise absolute blackness, four pinpricks of light
punctured the dark. His eyes slowly learned to read the blurred
shadows in front of him. Each light was a flame on a yellow candle. They formed a square in front of the royal chest. Hidden
within a thick fog of taper smoke, two white figures sat cross-
legged on the ground. One looked up angrily at the intruder.

"Good God, boy. What kept you?"

Phosy finally took a breath.

"Siri?"

"That's a relief. I was sure you were already a goner. Get your
bum over here. We need one more."

Phosy crunched over to the misty square of candles.

"I don't. . . ."

The second white figure was deep in prayer, oblivious to anything else.

"This," whispered Siri, "is Inthanet. He's going to open your
box for you. Sit yourself down."

Phosy, still high on fear, took in every detail of the surround-
ings. The music was playing loudly from an old cassette
recorder that sat on the workbench. The play button was obviously faulty. It was taped down with cellophane tape.

Between Siri and Inthanet was a white sheet spread on the
ground. It was stained red here and there from the severed head
of a pig and a small butcher's display of other dismembered internal organs. Phosy hoped they were animal. This orgy of blood was
set off prettily with bananas and mangosteen and young coconuts,
all laid out like decorations on a large wedding cake.

A tray holding a ceremonial banana-leaf cone sat atop the
chest. Other leaves fanned out from its base interspersed with
ripe banana slices. Four pairs of beeswax tapers, a cut flower,
and a stick of magic incense jutted from the cone-like quills.

Unspun cotton threads and pungent jasmine hung from the structure as if they'd fallen there by chance.

On the tray base were a silver knife, coins, and several brightly polished stones, and defying gravity at the apex of the cone sat an egg. Phosy had seen similar constructions often at weddings and birthdays and he knew there was to be a *basee* ceremony. But this one was much fancier than any he'd seen in his life.

"Siri, I. . . ."

"Shush. He's coming back."

Inthanet emerged from his prayer trance and seemed to notice Phosy for the first time, even though he'd been staring straight at him the whole time.

"How are you, son?" he asked.

"Fine."

Not true.

Inthanet took the egg from the cone and held it out to Phosy, who let it lay in his palm. The old man then lit the tapers from each of the four victory candles and held them between his palms. He caused the smoke to waft three times around the *basee* cone and once around Phosy's face. He passed the tapers to Siri who repeated the procedure while Inthanet recited a Pali incantation.

After a few minutes, Inthanet took hold of the *basee* tray with his right hand and Phosy's egg hand with his left. His eyelids flickered shut. Phosy raised his right hand with his palm facing his right ear. Siri returned the tapers to the cone and rested one hand on each man to complete the circuit. Inthanet continued to chant with a seriousness befitting the situation.

When he re-emerged from his trance, he took a thread from the cone. He dragged it three times across Phosy's wrist before looping and tying it there. The three men then took strings from the cone and continued to tie them around each other's wrists until all the thread was used up.

Inthanet, with one final flourish of language, took the egg from Phosy, broke it on the ground, and inspected the inside of the shell. It was unstained, almost perfect. He smiled at his co-mediums, and they knew the signs were good. Their leader removed the tray from the chest and laid his palm flat on the lid.

Mumbling quietly to himself, he slowly raised his hand. The lid creaked and lifted with it, as if his palm were a strong magnet. It was evidently powerful enough to raise even the eyebrows of the watchers. When the lid was open and leaning against the workbench, Inthanet looked down into the chest and smiled as if he were greeting old friends.

"So, how have you been, my lovelies?"

He nodded to Siri, who opened a bottle of rice whiskey that had been sitting amongst the road-kill on the sheet. He poured some into a plastic cup and handed it to Inthanet. He in turn knocked back one or two sips before filling his mouth with the remainder. He leaned over the casket and blew out a fine spray of the liquid through tight lips.

"There, that should wake you up."

Phosy was dying to take a look inside the chest, but he felt too much like a part of the ceremonial display to change his position. However, things soon became clear. While Siri lit a cigarette from one victory candle, Inthanet reached gently into the box and lifted out the leader of the Xiang Thong puppets. He was a pearl-faced prince in once-glittering robes. He was eighteen inches from the tip of his bare feet to the top of his winged helmet.

Inthanet took a second swig of whiskey and sprayed the puppet's face. It almost seemed to grin with its new shine. Siri had seen this face before. It had been in his dreams. He hadn't imagined it was a puppet. It had cheered from the roof as the ministry official plummeted to his death. It had danced for him and the king. It had looked down at Siri when he was trapped in the box. He realized now that he had been inside the royal chest looking out through the matte black eyes of these marionettes.

Siri handed the lighted cigarette to the old man, who took a drag and blew smoke into the prince's face. These indignities were apparently gestures of respect to the puppet spirits. Phosy thought how at-home they would be in some seedy puppet bar. The gesture was repeated lovingly for each of the forty figures.

He called them all by name and passed on funny anecdotes about them to his audience. He told of how the green-faced demon was a devil with the ladies. Once, the troupe had hired a particularly pretty puppeteer. On a number of occasions she would wake up in the morning to find the demon's white fangs smiling beside her on the pillow. The girl's door was always locked and there was no way for anyone to bring the demon into her room. She soon deserted the troupe.

Another puppet was a slim dancing girl with a pointed headdress. One day an old puppet master was so carried away with the drama of a scene that he accidentally let go of the puppet's stick as she was leaping. She soared up to the rafter and was embedded into the wood by her hat. She was soon rescued, but the indignity was too much for the dancing girl. The next morning, they found the puppet master wedged at the top of a tall *champac* tree with no recollection of how he had gotten there.

One, a smoking puppet, refused to go back into the chest unless he was allowed to take a puff of the cigarette himself with his big cheeks. The cigarette burned bright when it touched his lips and smoke came from the puppet's ears, even though he was as solid as soap.

Time seemed to be of no importance. When all the puppets were laid out across the workbench in neat rows, Phosy looked at his watch and realized the sun would soon be rising. The cigarettes had all been smoked. Two whiskey bottles lay on their sides empty. The final candle huffed its final sliver of gray smoke just as the lid of the chest was being shut.

"You won't have any more trouble with them," Inthanet sighed. "I don't know about you two, but I'm tuckered out. Can we go home now?"

The Inthanet Connection

The two white-haired men woke in a sweat at noon. It was the devil of a hot day without a whisper of a breeze to be had anywhere. It was the type of day that could wilt a metal gatepost. The only thing preventing Siri and Inthanet from waking earlier was the mental exertion of last night's ceremony. They were so drained, they could have slept through a house fire.

Siri looked over from his cot, Inthanet from his hammock.

"Hot, isn't it?"

"Damned hot."

They smiled and scratched and sat up.

"You'll be keen to get back to Luang Prabang now, I suppose," Siri said. In their brief time together, Siri and the old showman had become good friends.

"Not at all. Not at all. I'm sixty-eight, brother, and this is my first time away from the north. This is like winning the provincial lottery. How else would I get a free ride on my first-ever airplane? How else would I get to see the great southern capital and reside in a splendid mansion? This is the most fun I've had in decades. We found the puppets and got them settled and we pulled a magnificent fast one over your grumpy neighbor. All fun, Siri. All fun. I intend to drag this out for as long as I can. May even do a bit of sightseeing. In fact, you may never get rid of me."

"You know you're welcome to stay as long as you like. Just let me know when you've had enough, and I'll put you on the flight home."

"That's a deal."

Siri stared at his roommate and seemed to be weighing up just how close their friendship had become.

"Inthanet."

"Yes, brother."

"Could I ask a favor of you?"

"Certainly."

"It's quite an unusual one."

"As if this isn't wholly an unusual trip."

"Okay. Don't go away."

Siri went into the room where he had piled his clothes and fished his flashlight out of his pack. He came back to the cot where Inthanet now sat and plonked himself beside him.

"I want you to count my teeth."

Inthanet rolled back with laughter. When it eventually subsided and he realized this was no joke, he took the light and shined it into the doctor's open mouth.

"Wah, you certainly have a healthy looking set there, brother. I've lost most of mine, but this is quite a plantation. Do you mind if I use a finger? I don't want to lose count."

Siri could only gargle an okay, as the finger was already on the back molar and sliding around to the incisors on the bottom deck.

"But I suppose that's one of the benefits of living with nature all those years. No sweets to rot your teeth away. I'm a sucker for candy, I am. We used to give sweets to the kiddies who came to the puppet shows, but I ended up eating more than they did."

Siri wanted him to stop talking and concentrate on the counting. He didn't know anyone who could do both at the same time with any accuracy. The finger continued to trip along the row.

"I was going to get some of those false ones, but I thought better of it. I mean, you never really knew whose mouth they'd been in before yours or what they'd been chewing on. So I make do with the dozen I'm left with. Yours are beautiful, though. Just gorgeous. Better than a lot of young fellows."

He pulled out the finger and wiped it on his loincloth. "Sorry, I suppose I really should have washed this before I put it in your mouth. Still, no harm done."

"Did you count them?"

"Not much point being in there if I didn't, brother."

"How many have I got?"

"Thirty-three, brother. Thirty-three."

"You don't s . . . "

"Cooee." The sound of a woman calling them came not from outside the house, but from the back room a few feet away from where they sat on the porch.

"Anyone home?"

The men looked around to see the annoying Miss Vong in the back doorway.

"Yes, I thought I heard voices."

"Miss Vong, come in, why don't you?" Siri mumbled.

"Good morning, Mr. Inthanet."

"Good morning to you, Miss Vong."

They exchanged a warm smile that surprised Siri.

"You two are acquainted?"

"Of course," she said. "You abandoned the poor man on his first night here. He was all alone. He would have starved to death if it hadn't been for me."

"It's true, Siri. Miss Vong brought me a super home-cooked dinner, and she even cleaned up the place a bit."

"I'm sure she did."

"I've brought you two lonely bachelors another little treat. I just fixed up a batch of spicy minced fish."

As she went into painful detail of how she had prepared this unspectacular dish, Siri lamented the ground that had been lost. Over the previous month, he'd triumphantly reduced the number of charity housework invasions to a trickle. Now,

Inthanet's arrival had given her new incentive. Inthanet would have to go.

Her arrival also poured soapy water over his revelation. He had thirty-three teeth: him, Prince Phetsarath, and the Lord Buddha. He wanted to shout it. He wanted to celebrate without Miss Vong.

"Vong, this isn't the weekend, is it? Shouldn't you be at work?"

"Not this morning, comrade. We're off on a fact-finding mission to the southern provinces. We'll be traveling overnight, so we've got the morning off to pack."

His spirits rose.

"Will you be gone for many months?"

"Only four days. I'll be back before you know it. I'll take this into the kitchen and cover it." She walked inside with the bowl of fish *lahp*. In the distance they heard her say "Whoo, this kitchen could do with a good dusting."

"Not necessary, Miss Vong."

Siri and Inthanet smiled at each other and made faces as they probably had behind the teacher's back in primary school. Siri lowered his voice to ask: "What did you do with the dinner she brought you?"

"Not even your dog could get through it. I thought she might check the garbage can, so I gave it a decent burial over there under the papaya tree."

"Then I should abandon hope of papayas growing any time soon."

It reminded Siri he should dig up the machete before it started to rust. They laughed again and listened to the swish of the duster and the humming of a happy woman, born to clean.

It was as Siri was riding off on his motorcycle and Inthanet was closing the gate behind him that Mr. Soth, the neighbor, realized how cruelly he'd been cheated. He stood on a chair on his veranda and could see over the wall. There was a pair of them. He was mortified. How dare they? How dare anyone make fun of him?

Of course, it hadn't just been a case of mistaken identity. Inthanet had had to go to some effort to look like Siri. There was the walk of course, that tumbling forward walk that moved Siri around as fast as it did. But Inthanet had been a very fine actor in his day. There were some minor kapok additions to his eyebrows and the donning of Siri's favorite blue peasant suit, and Inthanet didn't even recognize himself. How could the neighbor know it wasn't Siri?

The doctor had seen Soth on the morning of the felling of the speaker pole. After all the secrecy and planning, it was infuriating to be caught red-handed in a suburb where not a soul wandered after midnight. He'd honed his machete to an edge so fine, it could slice through communist red tape. He'd figured on no more than ten swings to bring down the nasty speaker and he'd be back in his cot before the world was any the wiser.

How could he have taken account of mysterious Mr. Soth? How was he to know the man's habits? What right did he have to be awake at such an unhealthy hour? There was nothing to do in that place before dawn. But there he was, awake and brimming with vigilance.

On the flight from Luang Prabang, Siri and Inthanet had hatched this plot, along with several other contingencies. Dtui had told her boss on the phone about the visiting policemen and Tik, the old shaman, had been overwhelmed with a premonition of Siri rotting in jail. So Mr. Soth's initiative and Siri's arrest were both inevitable. The play was written and the action followed the script. But there was to be an unexpected last act.

Apart from being a creep, Mr. Soth was also a bad loser. He hadn't reached the economic heights and moral depths he occupied today by accepting humiliation. Revenge didn't have to be too complicated. A simple killing would do.

It was lunchtime, so Siri drove directly to the river, parked beneath a golden shower tree, and walked over to Civilai and

Phosy on their regular log. Both men were eating with their right hands and fanning themselves, geisha-like, with their left. The cheap Singha Beer logo fans from Thailand barely managed to slide the sweat across their foreheads. There was no natural movement in the air, and the river edged along so slowly it threatened to stop completely.

"Got anything to eat?" Siri asked.

"Will you listen to that." Civilai looked at Phosy without bothering to greet the newcomer. "The man makes over fifteen dollars a month, and he still has the gall to mooch off poor folk like us."

"Come on, you old miser. I know you've got a stash there in that bag."

Civilai reluctantly reached into the brown paper parcel and pulled out one of his wife's healthy sandwiches. Their bread habit had taken hold in France during their studies. Rightly or wrongly, but mostly wrongly, doughy white bread had been one of the few luxuries they'd dreamed of through their decades in the jungle.

Where the young men had baser, more animal priorities when sent to Hanoi for training or meetings, Siri and Civilai's first saliva-ridden thoughts were of crusty French baguettes and sumptuous fillings. They'd been delighted to see the cheap bread industry alive and well when they marched into Vientiane in '75, and proceeded to make up for time lost in the wilds of Houaphan.

"Hot, isn't it?"

"Damned hot."

"Damned hot."

"I've got thirty-three teeth."

"Don't be ridiculous."

"No, really, I—"

"I think this temperature's driving everyone a little batty," Civilai said.

"What's the latest?" Phosy asked.

"Well, top of the loony list is that most of the politburo are talking about banning festivals because they encourage spontaneity. 'Over my dead body,' I say. Then this morning, the Thai foreign minister announced that the Lao king, whom we all know is presently holidaying in the sunny wilds of Houaphan, was rescued from Luang Prabang by a crack Thai guerrilla unit and would see out his days on Thailand's sunny southern island of Phuket."

"I really do have—"

"Meanwhile, on the other side of the Pacific, the Yanks, following a brief experiment with enlightenment, have reintroduced corporal punishment. I think everyone needs to take a nice cold shower. I even got a peculiar phone call from your nurse this morning, Siri."

Siri was sulking and didn't respond.

"I'd settle for an air-conditioned office," Phosy lamented.

"The cutting room at the morgue's got AC," Siri reminded them. "You could both come and hang out there. I'd even let you—"

"I don't think we need to know, thanks."

"How's your body double?" Civilai asked.

"I can't think what you mean." Siri sat between the two men and unwrapped his lunch. "I personally don't see any similarity between Mr. Inthanet and myself. Do you, Inspector?"

"You're both conniving old bastards."

"I mean, physically."

"Come on, old fellow. We're waiting to hear about your friend and the complete royal puppet story."

"And a few missing details about last night," Phosy added.

Siri washed down a mouthful of bread with a swig from Phosy's iced coffee flask. The ice hadn't survived the day.

"Well, it isn't really that complicated, boys. older brother, do you think you could wave that thing a bit harder? It's hot here."

Civilai hit him with the fan.

"Thank you. Where should I start? When I was in Luang Prabang, I asked around about the chest I'd seen at the Ministry. When I described it, I was put in touch with our friend Inthanet. He was one of the five surviving keepers of the Royal Xiang Thong temple puppets. They'd been quiet for a while."

"I seem to recall that my cabinet banned them from using royal language in performances, and the puppets refused," Civilai grinned.

"That's right. The chest was ceremonially closed and stored at Xiang Thong. It was your classic puppet–politburo standoff. But the puppets had no intention of coming out, so it looks like the government went in after them.

"Some men in safari suits came one day and grabbed the chest. Nobody was sure who they were or where they were planning to take the puppets. The abbot charged with their safekeeping was shown a government directive that the chest was to be moved for security reasons. When the abbot asked for details, they told him it was all confidential. There wasn't much he could do about it.

"And that's how the chest ended up in the archive department of the Ministry and why all hell broke loose. You see, the chest can't be opened by just anyone whenever they feel like it. The spirits of the puppets are incredibly powerful and amazingly temperamental. They were already—"

"How can puppets have spirits?" Civilai interrupted.

"What?"

"Puppets aren't people, and they aren't dead. So how—?"

"Ah, but the puppets are made of balsa, and before the wood to carve them is cut from the tree, the puppet-maker has to get permission from the tree spirits. The balsa is a gentle wood and spirits are plentiful in it. When they learn that the wood is going to be made into the image of a person, it's awfully tempting for the more nostalgic spirits to jump ship and settle in the form of the puppet. It's as if they've returned to their lost host.

"The balsa spirits attract others to the puppets: dead puppeteers, artisans, dancers, until each one has a personality and a force of its own. Inthanet knows all of them and how to open and close the chest without offending them. When I told him I'd seen the royal seal on a box at the Ministry, he was only too pleased to come with me to Vientiane. He's quite a character. You'd like him, brother. He'd never been out of Luang Prabang in his life."

Phosy stood and walked toward the crest of the riverbank before it dropped steeply to the shallow river.

"All right. That explains who Inthanet is. Now let's cut to last night. I still have one or two little mysteries of my own to solve. When was this ceremony planned, may I ask?"

"Originally we weren't going to do it until the weekend. We'd booked a little orchestra, and they weren't free till Saturday."

"You booked an orchestra?"

"Just half a dozen traditional instruments. And we should have spent longer paying respect to local balsa trees. But you messed all those plans up with your impatience."

"Impatience? I'd been making excuses to my boss for a week."

"Patience shouldn't expire, son. Everything comes to he who waits."

"Especially early retirement."

"When I heard at Mahosot that you were on your way to open the chest, I knew you were in trouble. I raced home and picked up Inthanet and whatever paraphernalia he had ready. We were really pushing our luck with the cassette recorder. The spirits much prefer live music. We swung by a balsa copse and briefly explained what we intended, and got a sort of emergency go-ahead from the spirits there.

"All the time, I was picturing you, haunted by some angry spirits, leaping headfirst through the upstairs window. I was so relieved when we got there and didn't see your effeminate motor scooter parked nearby or your impatient body splattered in the road."

"I bet I could have made it all the way to the fountain. But, tell me, how did you get up to the seventh floor without going through the damned door?"

"Inthanet recited a magic mantra and spirited us up through time and space. I felt my body dissolve like sugar in water, and all the parts rose into the air. It was the most wonderful sensation. One minute we were at the fountain, the next we were with the chest."

They stared at him, open-mouthed.

"You can *not* be serious."

"No. Just kidding. We broke in through the side door on the ground floor." Civilai hit him again with the fan. "Then we used the other stairwell from the fifth to the seventh."

"What other stairwell?"

"Funny you, as a clever detective, didn't notice a whole staircase."

"There was no—"

"Certainly was. We came to the locked door and I thought we'd have to break it down. But Inthanet sensed there was another way. It was at the other end of the building, boarded off, didn't have a door. The hardboard was just glued on. It came away very easily. The stairs were riddled with white ant, but if you kept to the sides. . . . There was another board at the top."

"I'm embarrassed."

"No need to be. I'm sure the people working there had no idea either. It was probably boarded over long ago when the steps got dangerous. Now, give me a break. I'm getting hungry."

He smiled and took a large bite out of the sandwich.

"I guess I was lucky, then," Phosy decided. "Thank you. But you really should have told me what you had lined up."

"You're quite right," Siri chewed. "I apologize. But I was a little preoccupied with being arrested and put on trial."

"Darned lucky you weren't convicted to go with it," Civilai added.

"Surely you don't still believe I'm guilty."

"I tell you, younger brother, I certainly wouldn't want to live next door to that man after all the embarrassment you've caused him."

"Don't worry, Brother. I've met people like him before. They talk a lot, but deep down they're all cowards. I'm more afraid of living next door to Miss Vong. By the way, did I mention to anyone that I have thirty-three teeth?"

It was too hot to drag lunch out any longer, and Siri wheeled his motorcycle to the hospital parking lot. It was already around two, and he was feeling like a schoolboy who'd skipped classes for half a day. He hadn't seen Mr. Geung for over a week, and he hoped the poor fellow wasn't bogged down with bodies.

As he walked into the low concrete building, he called out in his friendliest voice: "Anybody in this morgue still alive?" There was no reply. "Hello?"

Mr. Geung came scurrying out of the office half in panic, half in relief at seeing Siri. He was too flustered to speak. He was rocking fit to roll over.

"Calm down, Geung. Calm down."

Siri led him back into the office, sat him down, and rubbed his shoulders till his breathing returned.

"Now, slowly."

"It . . . it . . . it's Dtui."

"Yes?"

"Shhh . . . she's dis . . . appeared."

Saloop, the lifesaver, had eaten a healthy rice-and-scrap lunch with his fiancée at the ice-works yard. The owners there liked him and encouraged him to hang around. He was different from the other dogs who seemed to only have one thing on their minds.

But today it was too hot to sit around and spoon and she wasn't in the mood for romance, so he took a leisurely stroll back home. He'd been enjoying the company of the man from the north and felt he should be there more to look after him. People were hopeless on their own.

He stopped to sniff at an occasional post and wall to make sure there were no interlopers in his territory. But sniffing stale urine on a full stomach in that heat naturally made him feel queasy. That's probably why his canine senses weren't as keen as usual. It probably explains why he didn't notice the movement in the yard before he smelled the scent. But the scent was unmistakable.

He hadn't had a great many opportunities to sample chocolate. It was a luxury so rare, they didn't even have any at the Lan Xang Hotel. Yet once, when he was a puppy, some rich foreign lady had given him just enough to get him hooked. He'd followed that lady for blocks until she shook him off, but the taste was with him for life.

He didn't get his second fix until fifteen years later when he and Siri moved out here to the suburbs. Those neighbors—the kids that ate better than the president—they had chocolate one day. The scent wafted through the air and pulled him by his nose out of a deep sleep. He went to their gate and saw them chewing on bars of the stuff. They teased and taunted him, pretending to give him some, then pulling it away.

It was more than he could take. He feigned a loss of interest, coiled the inside of his neck like a spring then just as the boy was about to pull the bar away he snapped at it. The kid only just got his fingers away in time. He dropped the bar and Saloop strode off with it, victorious. The children ran inside to tell their mother of the vicious dog that attacked them and took their chocolate.

That was a fortnight ago, and he'd been waiting for a chance to get back into his new drug of choice. This was it. Their gate was open and one of the kids had left a half bar of chocolate right there in the middle of the path, melting under the hot sun. It was too easy. He'd probably be as sick as a . . . well, he'd probably be sick, but anyone who's ever suffered an addiction knows you can't fight it.

He walked slowly along the rock pathway, listening carefully for movement inside the house, but not many people were planning on coming out into the sun on a day like this. And suddenly it was under his nose. He sniffed at its glorious milky sweetness, let his tongue dip into the gooey paste and slurped it up.

Life didn't get any better than this: a house in the suburbs, a caring master, the love of a good bitch, and chocolate. For a second he wondered if he'd ever been happier.

"A fat one?"

"She is quite large, I suppose."

"Yeah. She was here. You know where she works?"

"Why do you need to know?"

"For the RR29."

"RR29?"

"It's the regulation complaint form that accompanies official telephone calls to law enforcement departments."

"What did she do?"

"Illegal access to government documents. They said I'd need to find out where she works before they can do anything—especially seeing as she didn't technically steal anything. So, do you?"

The man sat at a small desk in a room so crammed with piles and boxes of papers, one match would have sent the whole building to ashes in minutes.

So, this was it, Siri thought to himself looking at the vaguely Chinese features of a face slowly adopting the shape and color of a sheet of paper. This was what all the triplicates and quadruplicates came to. Hundreds of officious cadres like this, processing endless documents by hand, passing them on to other paper-faced clerks in other offices, and filing them away in rooms like this. What a system.

This was the filing section of the Department of Corrections. The only appointment marked in Dtui's log for today was:

8:30 CORRECTIONS

"So, do you?"

"Do I what?"

"Know where she works."

"No. I have no idea."

"Then how did you know she was here?"

"You just told me."

"But why here, at Corrections?"

"It was next on my list. We're investigating her. She's tried this kind of thing before."

"Who's we?"

Siri produced his well-thumbed letter of introduction from the Justice Department. He was learning that in most cases, just having a document was enough to get him into places. Few bothered to read the long stodgy wording. The letterhead was enough. The clerk sensed he was already involved in a matter of intrigue.

"What's she done, then?" the clerk asked.

"She goes around impersonating a nurse, you know, goes into this department and that, claiming this and that."

"Damn. I knew there was something fishy about her. Didn't look like any nurse I'd ever seen."

"Suppose you tell me what happened."

The filing clerk was visibly excited. His dull life desperately needed days such as these.

"She marches in here as if she owns the office and says Dr. Vansana asked her to come and look up something in the files. Dr. Vansana's the physician we use at the correctional facilities. I mean, ha, as if anyone can just march in and claim to be this or that and get access to my files. I mean, she didn't have so much as a P124."

"You can't be serious."

"I jest you not, comrade. Well, Dr. Vansana's off at the reservoir today so there wasn't even any way of checking her story. I wasn't letting her get her hands in my drawers, I can tell you."

"I don't blame you."

"Right. So she kicked up a fuss and I told her I wasn't even supposed to be talking to her till I saw an Int5Q, so she should go away and come back with some paperwork. I asked her, 'Where do you think the country would be if everyone conducted his or her daily business without the correct forms?'"

"Good for you."

"I can't even tell you what she said to that. I said 'Good day' and went back to my deskwork. She stormed out, and I suppose I eventually calmed down and forgot about her. I found myself engrossed in a rejac. budg. requisition that needed some back-up R11's. I'm a bit short-staffed right now. Normally I'd have a girl running back and forth to the cabinet room for files, but these days I'm having to do it myself. So I went next door and what do you know? The door was locked. I banged and banged and who should come to the door?"

"I think I know."

"Her, brazen as anything, comes and opens the door. And she has the nerve to tell me she took a wrong turn and got herself locked in that room with the files. A likely story I do not think. I mean, the lock's on the inside for the first thing, and there she was opening it. I was flabbergasted. I'd never seen such abuse of the regulations.

"Of course, what I should have done at that point was restrain her and call for security, the police even. But, well, she was a big girl and I'm not a physically well person, so I instructed her to leave, forthwith. Would you believe she strolled past me smiling without a glimmer of guilt?"

"I would." He fought back his own smile.

"What?"

"I mean, she's a hardened criminal. These people have no shame. Too bad you don't know what file she was looking at."

"Ha. Not know? You don't think I could spend over a year setting up this system and not know what's been tampered with? She didn't even bother to put it back in the drawer straight. DC19368.3. That, comrade, is a criminal record file."

"I wish all our witnesses were as diligent as you, comrade. I'm afraid I'll have to take a look at that file. It's the only evidence we have against her."

"What's her name?"

"Her name? We refer to her as . . . as HJJ838."

The man jotted it down.

Twenty minutes later, Siri walked out of the Corrections Department into a brick wall of dry heat. It had to be the hottest damned year he'd ever known. There hadn't been more than a sneeze of rain since last December. Nothing was really green anymore.

A depleted flock of bicycle taxi pedalers wilted on their back seats beneath the gray leaves of a peacock-tail tree.

"Good health," Siri said hopefully.

"Good health, uncle," a couple replied. They'd seen him arrive on his motorcycle, so they knew there was no chance of a fare.

"Hot, isn't it?"

"Damned hot."

"I don't suppose any of you recall giving a ride to a nurse here this morning, do you? About nine?"

"I do," said a bare-chested young man with a stack of coat hangers inside his skin. "There was a heavy one this morning. It was me that took her."

"Remember where to?"

"Out to Silver City, uncle. Almost killed me it did, day like this."

"Thank you."

Siri was on his way back to his bike when he glanced across

the street. In the heat that shimmered up from the pavement, he saw Saloop sitting with his long tongue flopping out of his mouth.

"Saloop?" Siri said. "What the heck are you doing here?"

He remembered the old Lassie black and white films he'd seen at Le Ciné in Paris. Perhaps his dog had come to tell him there was danger back at the house. He couldn't think how he'd traced him here. He waited for an old Vietnamese truck to pass before going across to see. But once the vehicle and its trailer of tarry black smog had cleared the lane, Saloop had gone.

"I never will get that dog," Siri said to himself.

Getting Warmer

Before the Silver City trip, Siri stopped off at the morgue to see whether Dtui had made an appearance. All he found was Geung sweeping grooves into the concrete floor. At the hospital administration office, Siri called Phosy and by a one-in-a-hundred chance found him at his desk. He told Siri about the appointment he'd completely forgotten the previous evening with Dr. Vansana. He also told him to call back if Dtui still hadn't shown up by five. It was already nearly four.

There was one more stop before Silver City. He arrived at the ugly shanty behind the high wall of the national stadium and walked along the narrow dirt lane, wading through a flock of newborn chicks. At Dtui's banana-leaf door, he called out Manoluk's name before going in.

"Ooh, come in, Doctor. Haven't seen you for ages."

Dtui's mother lay as always on the thin mattress in the center of the room. The head of the standing fan cluttered and groaned back and forth but did a poor job of lowering the temperature in the stuffy slum. She'd never looked well in all the time Siri had known her, but she'd looked a lot worse than she did today. He didn't want to distress her by discussing Dtui's disappearance.

"Good health, Mrs. Manoluk. How you feeling?"

"Just fine," she lied. "What brings you?"

"I was visiting the family of one of our deceased around here," he lied back. "Thought I'd drop in and see how you're doing."

He reached into his shoulder bag for his traveling doctor kit.

"Actually, I haven't been in the morgue all day. I hope Dtui's looking after the show for me."

"Must be, Doctor. She left here bright and early this morning. Can't think where else she'd be, unless she took off across the river."

This was a long-standing joke in Vientiane. If so-and-so was late or his brother missed a day at work, they'd talk about him taking a swim to Thailand. It was only partly said in jest, as there were very few of the population of 150,000 who hadn't given it a thought.

"No plans to go and have her hair done, manicure?"

"Goodness me, no. Can you imagine Dtui with a permanent wave?"

Damn. So, whatever came up was sudden and unplanned. Before leaving, as was his habit, he gave the old woman a check-up. They chatted, and he left some herbal tea to help her sleep. There were the constant cries of babies, the yelling of neighbors, the dogs. He wasn't sure tea would help her sleep through that. He really needed to get her into a better place.

Warmer Still

He was on his motorcycle, heading at last to Silver City. It was like riding into the blast of a hair-dryer set on hot. The sweat that had soaked him at Manoluk's dried the moment he stepped out into the sunshine. Now his shirt was burning his skin. The heat didn't help his troubles at all. There was one thing he couldn't get out of his mind. Dtui was one of the world's great carers. She knew about Geung's condition and that he'd be frantic with worry about her. She wasn't the type to be away all day without getting word back to him. Siri was sure something had happened to her.

For the first time, his wrinkled letter didn't impress the guards at the gate of the Secret Police HQ one little bit. The man on his stepladder looked down through the peep hatch and read it while Siri held it up to him.

"No. Nothing to do with us. Sorry, comrade. Can't let you in."

After a good deal of contrived pouting and hammering and threatening from the doctor, the guard brought his commanding officer who, in turn, brought Mr. Phot, the interpreter. They still wouldn't let Siri inside, but they did allow Phot to go out and talk to him. He brought out a large white parasol and opened it over their heads.

"What exactly have you got in there that's so top secret?" Siri asked.

"Mystery," was the reply. "People always need to think there's something going on. It keeps them on their toes. If the proletariat knew we didn't actually have any secrets, they wouldn't respect us nearly as much." Siri smiled. "So, you're Dtui's boss. She told me about you."

"Has she been here today?"

"It was a flying visit."

"Can you tell me what she wanted?"

"Don't see why not. It was about something the Russian had started to say on her first visit. She hadn't really taken much notice then, or perhaps I didn't do a very good job of translating. He'd made a comment about the teeth marks."

"The tiger's?"

"He was sure it was some type of cat. A tiger was the most likely candidate. But there was something odd about them."

"What kind of odd?"

"He said he'd never seen such sharp canines before. The indentations almost ran to a point. It was almost as if they'd been deliberately sharpened."

"Sharpened? Why would anyone want to do that, and how?"

"Good questions, Doctor. But it certainly makes the creature you're looking for one scary old foe, don't you think?"

They both stood reflecting on that for a few seconds.

"Hot, isn't it?"

"Damned hot."

Getting Cooler

As he'd heard, Dr. Vansana was off at the reservoir. Siri sat in the back yard of his house downwind from a simply enormous fan that Sam, the doctor's wife, had dragged out from inside. It was about three feet across and felt something like flying behind an Antonov 12. He had to hold his lemon tea with both hands.

"This is the coolest I've felt all day," he yelled above the growl of the motor.

"I'm so glad you aren't one of those vain men who wears a toupee. It would be in Nong Kai by now," his hostess said.

He laughed, but she could tell he was deeply worried about Nurse Dtui.

"I just wish there was more I could do to help. I think I've told you everything we talked about last night."

"But your husband was convinced this Seua fellow wasn't the mass murdering type?"

"Absolutely. Vansana was quite disturbed after Dtui left, in fact. He was certain she was on the wrong track. But she seemed so convinced there was a connection. And to make matters even worse, she thought that connection might be supernatural. I'm afraid my husband doesn't hold with that kind of talk. He's a scientist."

"Yes. I used to be, too. I can understand his feelings. Did she give you any idea of where she was planning to go today, apart from the Corrections Office?"

"That was it, I'm afraid. She mentioned she wished she knew more about spirits and werewolves. Nothing else."

"Sorry, do you have a telephone?"

"Yes, Doctor. The regime kindly let us keep ours. The neighbors weren't so lucky. Thank goodness Vansana's a medical man."

Siri tried to get through to Civilai and Phosy. Both were out of the office and neither had left messages to say when or if they'd be back. It was five already, and the last time anyone had seen Dtui was around ten that morning. He went off to the Police Department to file a missing persons complaint even though, without Phosy's personal attention, he didn't have much faith in the ability of the police force to find her.

Where had she gone after Silver City? What was preventing her from phoning or coming back? Perhaps she'd had an accident. For the moment, her trail had gone cold.

Freezing

She couldn't believe how cold it was in that place when the air outside was so hot. Or perhaps it was just a nervous reaction to fear. She felt down the front of her uniform. It was caked in some kind of mud. Some of it was hard. It occurred to her it might have been her own blood. There was no way of telling. There were certainly injuries.

She'd been thrown to the ground and dragged like a sack of black beans and left where she now sat. Her chest, her face, her thighs were bruised and possibly bleeding. There was no light, not a trickle. The treacly blackness, the thin bad-tasting air, and the noises, these were the devils that made her physical health seem unimportant. They slowly added layer by layer to the horror of what she had stumbled upon.

There was nothing she could do but sit with her back against the wall and listen. Back and forth it paced, panting and shuffling and gurgling from its throat. Then there was the smell. She'd been in the morgue long enough to recognize death, but this was more. The blood and the death mingled with the creature's own stink as if it were a part of it.

She had never feared more for her life. She could never have been more certain that this was her last day, and it was her own stupid fault. Why, she wondered at first, was she still alive when all the others had been killed instantly? But as her mind cleared, the reason became obvious. This was the final day of the solstice when the moon would be at its fullest. The others had been killed over the five days leading up to this night. The beast was waiting for that moon to rise before taking its final sacrifice. In a few hours, she would be just like the other women, except here in this cold black place nobody would ever find her body.

Weretiger

It wasn't until he arrived at Hay Sok temple that Siri realized he didn't know the name of the monk he'd come to find. The moon was rising fast, and the temple grounds stood out in its light like the national stadium under floodlights.

He walked around the inside of the whitewashed wall until he got to the stretch that had been blown up the previous year, along with his house. The monks had done a good job of fixing it. There was no longer a hole to look through; but by standing on the incinerator, he could see the far side. The ruins of his former house still lay there. The rubble hadn't been collected, and the side wall still warped and leaned inward. All but one, they'd been lucky to get out before the place collapsed.

"Are you up there thanking your lucky stars, Yeh Ming?"

The monk stood behind him, his pate freshly shorn. He wore his saffron wrap as a loincloth. In the moonlight, Siri noticed the rings of tattooed mantras around his upper arms and across his chest. It perhaps explained his magical abilities. Somehow the monk knew all about Siri and Yeh Ming. It was he who had rescued the white talisman, he who had predicted that Dtui's mother would have a better year.

"I am that," Siri smiled. "It's been a while. How have you been?"

He sat down on top of the incinerator.

"You'll eventually come to understand that luck and coincidence aren't connected. It wasn't a coincidence that your dog

led you away from the house that night. It was no coincidence
that the Indian tackled your policeman friend last evening."

Siri laughed.

"Is there anything you don't know?"

"Oh, yes. So many things, but not those things that concern
you, Yeh Ming."

"Who are you exactly?"

"You don't need to know that. I see you're wearing the talisman."

In fact he could see no such thing, not with his eyes anyway.
It was around the doctor's neck beneath his shirt.

"It makes my skin itch."

"You were fortunate in Luang Prabang. Didn't I tell you to
wear it always?"

"I was always poor at taking advice. But I think I get the idea
now."

"Good. What brings you here?"

"I thought you were all-seeing, all-knowing."

"Only in spiritual matters."

It was an odd comment that Siri would come to dwell on later.

"What do you know about weretigers?"

"More than I care to." He walked over and joined Siri on the
incinerator. "A weretiger is a tiger spirit that can from time to
time possess the soul of a woman or man."

"And vice versa?"

"What do you mean?"

"Could it be a man who turns into a tiger?"

"We are talking about spirits, Yeh Ming. Spirits don't turn
people into animals. They may make them believe they are this
or that beast, but there's no physical manifestation."

Siri was taken aback.

"What? What about werewolves?"

The monk laughed.

"I'd say you have wasted too many hours watching motion
picture films."

It was true. Siri and Boua had sat through many hours of Lon Chaney with a face like a chihuahua biting into the necks of unsuspecting village folk. Given all that had happened to Siri over the last fifteen months, the least he expected was a parade of ghouls and monsters.

"Then explain this," he said. "A man is released from Don Thao. He claims to be the host of a weretiger. A few days later comes the first of three killings, all showing evidence of a tiger's bite and scratch marks."

The monk looked perplexed.

"I cannot."

"Is there a possibility?"

"As it indeed happened, there has to be a possibility. But in all these years, I've never seen or heard of such a thing."

Siri shook his head and looked up at the huge moon.

"Do you think there could be a connection with the moon?"

"When did the killings take place?"

"The first was on the eighth. Then the tenth and eleventh."

"The moon isn't symbolic of spirit activity, but it is a great source of energy that unleashes a number of innate abilities and quirks. There are theories that the full moon can trigger electrical impulses in the mind. Not all insanity is connected to evil spirits."

"Where do they hang out? Weretigers."

"You mean apart from within the souls of humans?"

"Yes."

"When they aren't of this world, the Hmong believe they go to the other earth. It is a landscape not unlike the mountains they live their mortal lives on."

"How do they get there?"

"You enter the other earth through holes in the ground or networks of caves. These lead you to a great body of water where spirits and humans can converse. It's there that the supreme God, Nyut Vaj, decides whether you are eligible to enter the eternal Kingdom or whether you will have to float in purgatory."

"I see. So all I have to do is find the other earth and I'll have our friend, Mr. Seua."

Siri climbed down from the incinerator and reached out a hand to the nameless monk, who ignored the gesture.

"Yeh Ming . . . ?"

"Yes?"

"There's no doubt these people were killed by a tiger?"

"Or some other large cat."

"Then have you considered the possibility it was a real tiger?"

"We thought about it. But how could a wild cat run free in Vientiane without somebody seeing it?"

"What if it isn't free?"

"You mean if it's captive? It belongs to someone?"

"Do you know anyone who keeps wild animals?"

Siri's mind raced to Dtui's report of her visit to the circus school. He thought of the Russian and his puma. He had a mental image of the trainer late at night walking his big cat at the end of a leash. It was far-fetched but perhaps the only logical explanation, unless the monk was wrong about weretigers and werewolves. Surely Hollywood hadn't made it all up.

"I may. And that reminds me. If there's no such thing as a coincidence, I have one more for you to explain. I believe a bear might have sought me out and paid me a visit last Tuesday morning. Is there any connection between Yeh Ming and wild animals?"

"There's an inseparable connection between Yeh Ming and all nature. Animals sense that."

As he walked from the temple, one thought nagged at him. At Silver City, the interpreter had told him Dtui hadn't been there long. He had said it was a flying visit. What if he'd been lying? But why would he? And what could Siri do if he had? The compound was a fortress, and he had no pretext to get inside. He was flustered and anxious and in such a state he couldn't think as clearly as he'd like.

As it was close, he stopped again at Dtui's room. He was disappointed but not surprised to learn that she hadn't come home. So as not to worry Manoluk, he told her they had a case that might go on all night. He brought her a meal from the night stalls on Koonboulom and administered her medication. He did his best to appear calm; but all the while, his thoughts were on Dtui and what could have become of her.

He was in the back, searching for a glass into which to transfer the guava juice from its plastic bag. He pulled back a cloth on a low shelf and was surprised to find a row of textbooks. He squatted down and looked at the titles. They were in English but the words were similar enough to French to get the drift: *Fundamentals of Surgery, Chemical Toxicology, Oncology, Urology, Basics of Nursing.* Then there were dictionaries: English–Lao–English, English–Russian. And every book was twice as fat as it should have been because the pages were crammed with notepaper.

He selected the *Surgery* text. In Dtui's tiny handwriting, on every page there was a detailed description in Lao, and presumably a translation in Russian. There must have been thousands of such sheets. Siri was overwhelmed for a number of reasons. He walked across to Manoluk with the textbook in his hand.

"Manoluk, does Dtui understand English?"

"She didn't in the beginning. I think she's got the hang of it now. She only reads and writes it. Can't speak much. The problem's going to be the Russian. She has to learn the whole thing again in a new language."

"You think she actually knows what it all means?"

She gave him a look reserved for mothers whose daughters have been insulted.

"No, I didn't mean it to sound like that. She's an intelligent girl. But this stuff is hard enough in our native language. Learning it in two others is unbelievable. How long's she been doing this?"

"Since before she graduated as a nurse. She originally planned to try for a scholarship to America. That was in the old regime and there were a lot of dollars around. So she started going through her old nursing textbooks, translating line by line. Then you folks came and took over, and all the American funds went out the window. So she started all over again with Russian."

"I think she might have told me."

"Well, she—"

"What?"

"She was afraid that if anyone knew she had other languages, they'd move her from the morgue."

"And what's wrong with that?"

"Well, one, she got to like the work you do there. I think she'd like to be a, what do you call it?"

"Forensic surgeon."

"That's it. And two, you don't actually have a lot of work in the morgue. Nothing's so urgent that it can't wait till morning. It's a sort of eight-to-five job. She knows if she worked in the wards, they'd put her on shifts and get her translating and stuff. She wouldn't have time for her study. She's at it every night. She writes out little test sheets in Lao so I can test her, though I don't really have any idea what it's all about. She's the one with the brains in this family."

"So it seems."

Dtui never failed to amaze him. All this time, she'd been preparing herself for further study, even before he recommended her for a scholarship. What he'd thought was an act of kindness on his part was actually the inevitable fulfillment of her plan. She was studying overseas with or without his help.

"Manoluk, we should talk about this again, but right now I have something urgent that needs taking care of. I'm going to have to run."

He returned the textbook, gave Dtui's mother her juice, and headed for the door.

"Thanks for coming in. Tell Dtui not to worry about me."

"I will."

He felt overwhelmed. As he shut the clunky door that didn't fit its frame, tears came to his eyes. They were tears for Dtui and her dreams, and for her mother and her lifetime investment in her daughter. And they were tears of helplessness. Where on earth could he look next?

That's when he remembered something Civilai had said.

Despite constant prodding and poking from the Party, Civilai had still managed to avoid installing a telephone in his house.

"If they want me that urgently, let them get out of bed and come and get me," he said.

Siri and the bike trailing his pulled up in front of the wooden bungalow in the sprawling compound that had once housed the American community. If it weren't for the vegetation, you'd swear you were in a suburb in South Dakota. The LPRP had been only too delighted to take over this little piece of Americana and thumb their noses at the CIA who were now confined to a couple of rooms at the embassy.

Six Clicks, as the Americans christened their home away from home, was six kilometers from town. It had a pool and a gymnasium and restaurants and was surrounded by a large wall that could make the expats forget they were in a nasty Southeast Asian country far from home.

As always, one of the armed guards from the main gate had accompanied Siri, just in case he had an urge to detour and assassinate the prime minister. He'd been here hundreds of times, and they still didn't trust him. Siri beeped his horn.

Civilai appeared at the window and gestured for his friend to come in. His sweet wife appeared beside him and waved. Siri waved back but made no effort to get down from his bike. He pointed to his watch. Civilai had no choice but to come out to the street.

"We're both over the hoof-and-mouth disease. You could come in, you know."

"Sorry. I can't stop. In fact, if you had a phone, I would have preferred to do this without the Six K's."

"Good, that. Coming from a man who only learned how to use a telephone last year. What's so urgent?"

Siri looked at the guard and raised his eyebrows at Civilai, who dismissed the man. "It's all right. He's safe. You can go."

The guard roared away, and Civilai came over to sit on his white front fence.

"You said at lunch you had a call from Dtui this morning."

"And I thought you never listen to me."

"It's important, brother. She's been missing all day."

"Shit."

"What was the call about?"

"Like I said, it was quite peculiar. She wanted to know whether there were any underground caverns or caves around the city."

"You're joking. How did she . . . ? What did you tell her?"

"Well, do you recall the PL had its headquarters not far from the Black Stupa? It was just down from the U.S. compound. We used it as a base here till we took over."

"Yeah."

"We were always expecting to get attacked or kicked out. So we took a leaf out of the Viet Cong's survival manual. We gave ourselves a number of escape options."

"Tunnels?"

"That's it. There's quite a network down there."

"Damn."

"What is it?"

"Do any of those tunnels go in the direction of the river?"

"Of course. The water was the best way to get away at night. One of them actually passes directly under the French embassy."

"How do you get access?"

"What are you hatching?"

"Just tell me."

"Behind the main building, there's an area covered with large paving stones. One of those stones has a small hole in one corner. You need a hook or some kind of jemmy. It lifts up."

"Did you tell Dtui that?"

"Yes."

"Okay. Listen. Go find someone with a phone."

"What is it?"

"I think Dtui found those tunnels and something happened to her down there. The best we can hope for is that she got herself lost. But I'm afraid she might have found our weretiger."

"Our weret . . . ?"

"Tell Phosy to get some men there, armed, as soon as he can. If he's not around, call in the bloody army. I don't care what it takes."

He kicked the starter of his old bike.

"Where are you going?"

"Where do you think?"

"Siri, you do realize if she is down there with some animal or lunatic, she could already be. . . ."

"I know. I'm putting my money on Dtui."

He left eight inches of rubber on the road.

Blind Panic

The creature that Seua had become sat on the riverbank watching the moon rise. He scratched at the blood-caked fur that covered him in patches and dipped his face into the muddy water to quench his thirst.

It would soon be over for another month. The nurse would be the last. With the moon at its zenith, he would make his fourth sacrifice on the steps of the Black Stupa. He would dedicate it to Nyut Vaj. It couldn't be long, with all this love he showed, all this dedication, before his God would accept him into the Eternal Kingdom. Then he would be at peace and cease to walk the earth in animal form.

He looked up again. It was time. Bent almost double, he prowled to the spot where the roots of the sadness tree tangled down the bank. He parted the thick reeds and crawled deep between the roots and into the earth.

Siri was in such a state when he arrived at the old PL headquarters compound that he almost drove into a pole out front. He skidded to avoid it and only righted himself at the last second. He killed the engine and ran to the gate. It was chained shut, and even with all the extra adrenaline pumping through his veins, too high to climb over.

He reached inside and felt around the chain for a padlock. There was none. The chain had been draped around the bars and tied like a rope. He wrestled it loose, opened the gate wide enough to get inside, and barged through. His heart was already beating fast when he started to run down the side of the main building and around to the back.

There he found himself on a grid of large rectangular concrete slabs. The moon was high and bright, and it didn't take him long to find the secret entrance to the tunnel. He didn't even need to use a tool to raise it; someone had been there before him and left the slab lying beside a gaping hole in the ground.

He hurried to it and looked down into a pit. A ladder of steep wooden steps led down into inky blackness. He had no hesitation: He lowered himself into the hole and, with his feet, felt his way down the rungs. The thought of sinking down into the earth reminded him of his being dragged below the stupa by the *Phibob* and without thinking, he stopped, undid the top buttons of his shirt, and re-hung the white talisman so that it was on the outside.

When the top of his snowy head was at the level of the ground, he reached into his shoulder bag for the flashlight. It was always there, so he hadn't bothered to check before he left home. He never took it out, except on days when he got his teeth counted. His heart dropped. He'd forgotten to return the damned thing. It was missing.

It was a terrible moment. He was about to go down into the earth to find Dtui. He instinctively knew that every second could be vital, but he had no light. What help would he be if that thing were down there? At least the beam of a flashlight might have made it wary of him. How could he help if he couldn't see? Suddenly a difficult project had entered the realm of the impossible. But there was no time and no choice.

After two more steps, his feet landed on packed earth and he glanced upward at the moon one more time before turning away from the ladder. It was hopeless. Only a yard from where he stood, there was nothing to be made out with the naked eye. There were no shadows or shapes. The channel of moonlight ended at a wall of black.

Again he fumbled in the bag, this time to retrieve the motorcycle tire iron he'd brought to lift up the concrete. It was a small weapon that could have little effect against the power he'd seen evidenced on his morgue slab. But it was something to hold on to, like a stick to a blind person: a cattle prod between himself and the unseen.

He walked forward. The walls curved over and above him to become a ceiling just above his head. A man of average height would have had to stoop through this narrow passage, but Siri could stand to his full height. He dragged his left hand along one wall and could tap the opposite wall with the iron: such was the width.

After ten slow, cautious paces, the tunnel curved to the left and any evidence of light from the outside was erased. Behind him now lay the same tarry blackness as ahead. He was blind. It was at this point that an anxiety of sorts began to infect him. It arose from his foolishness in abandoning logic and safety. He could make neither head nor tail of what he was doing. In the jungle, he wouldn't have survived if he had showed such flagrant disregard for common sense.

He walked on. His dragging hand picked up a load of passengers that bit him and crawled up into his sleeve: probably red ants defending a nest. He slapped them off quietly against his side but didn't slow his pace. The air was becoming staler. The dry earth and musty root smells mixed with other less natural, less healthy scents. He had no doubt that something had died down there in those tunnels, and he hoped beyond hope it was an animal.

On he went, slowly, nervously.

The tip of the iron struck only air. Siri stopped and felt the far wall with his hand. A second tunnel. It cut to the right. How far had he already veered left? Which route would take him in the direction of the river? He waited for a sign. Surely with all the bodies he'd put in the ground, one grateful spirit could come along and prod him in the right direction. But there was just him, and the blackness, and silence. Nothing more.

He went right, increasing his pace as his instincts warned him about time. He knew he had to get to the river. He was no longer careful about what his hand might touch or what might lie under his feet. He visualized a long, well-lit passage and marched along it, barely tapping with his iron.

When it hit him, it was so sudden and overwhelming that he panicked. It had quickly wrapped itself around him, covered his face. He flailed around, hit out with the iron bar, and fell back against the wall, kicking into space.

He clawed at the cold, thick accumulation around his mouth and neck and cleared space enough for an unrestricted breath. Still he swung his iron back and forth like a child in an imaginary sword fight, but he hit nothing, heard nothing, and soon understood that he was expending all his energy against himself.

He held up a hand and stepped forward. He had come to a thick barrier of spiderwebs that blocked the tunnel ahead.

If this was a test, it was a failed one. He waited for his breath and his heartbeat to cease their rantings, and de-webbed himself. He wondered whether he'd made too much noise fighting off his fictitious attacker—whether he'd been heard. He couldn't be sure.

He quickly retraced his path to the main tunnel, turned right and proceeded somewhat more cautiously into it. Time hadn't allowed his eyes to grow accustomed to the darkness, so he knew there was absolutely no light filtering into the tunnels. He had completely lost his sense of direction. In a straight line, a brisk walk from the compound to the river would take no more than five minutes. To an old man in a pitch-black tunnel, a minute can stretch to a significant portion of the remainder of your life. The tunnel seemed endless.

Suddenly, the ground wasn't there anymore. Siri stepped into empty space, and only his guiding left hand against the wall prevented him falling arse over apex. He pulled himself back, got to his knees and reached down into the void with his iron. It was no bottomless chasm, just a deep step. The metal clunked against something solid but not heavy, then once more. The smells around him were overly familiar, but he had no choice but to step down into whatever was there.

He waded ankle-deep through a well of what he was sure were bones. They crunched beneath his feet, so they were small and not all fresh. Yet with every step he dreaded treading on a larger corpse. Because of this threat, he trod respectfully, with his breath held.

When he finally arrived at something solid, it proved to be no more than the step on the far side. He remembered the geography of the Viet Cong cave networks and wondered whether this was a pivot room. If it were, there would be tunnels leading off in each direction. Matters would become even more confusing if he had too many alternatives, so he didn't bother to find out. He continued going straight. He climbed the far step and set off again into the tunnel. But things soon went horribly wrong.

Late the previous year, after rescuing his neighbors from their ruined house, Siri had been hospitalized until the masonry dust could be cleared from his lungs. Although the dust was eventually flushed out, the air didn't ever return with the same enthusiasm. Consequently, the doctor started to find himself short of breath at the worst possible times. But none of those times had been as inopportune as now.

The further he moved from the only obvious source of oxygen, the deeper he had to trawl for air. He knew he had to concentrate on his breathing. The attack of the spiderweb had taken a lot out of him and he was now in danger of blacking out. If he lost consciousness, this whole horrible ordeal would have been a waste of time.

He stopped, lay down on the ground where the richer air would still be, and gently meditated himself into a more relaxed state. He ignored the slithering and crawling around his head, and concentrated on replenishing his energy.

This was when he began to hear, or believed he could hear, sounds. They were muffled, far off, and could, for all he knew, have been coming from above the tunnels rather than within them. But this was late at night in Vientiane. There wouldn't be much activity in the streets. He listened intently.

At first he didn't recognize it. The noise was sporadic and muted like a bee in a tin can. He wasn't able to identify it as either natural or man-made. But the longer he listened, the more obvious it became to him that the sound was getting louder. If it was in the tunnels, it could mean only one thing. It was coming toward him.

He told himself not to panic, reminded himself he had the element of surprise. But surprise on whom or on what? Some surprise it would be, with him flat out in the middle of a narrow passage. And what if there were no connection between this noisemaker and Dtui's disappearance? Was he really considering laying into some stranger with an iron bar just because he was scared out of his wits?

Yes.

"Don't panic," he told himself. He breathed. He lay still. He thought calm thoughts, and the sounds got louder—not a buzz now, but a growl. Now and again the growl would rise to a howl, a human–animal high-pitched roar, and it came to him:

This was the sound from his dream in Luang Prabang. This was the unseen danger that approached through the jungle, the sound that he was to listen for in the future, to avoid, to flee with every iota of strength he possessed. He shuddered, and his nerve endings tingled the length of his body.

Still he focused. Still he breathed. No sort of attack or defense would be possible if he were unconscious. He devised a plan. When he had enough breath to carry it through, he would return to the room through which he'd just passed. There were corners there, perhaps other tunnels. These could give him a chance.

Because of the natural deadening effect of the earthen walls, it wasn't possible to tell just how far off the creature was. But from the steady increase in volume, it was evident that it was traveling at a rapid pace.

Siri breathed. He concentrated. He heard other sounds. He heard footsteps, heavy shuffling steps, and, between the howls and grunts, a heavy wheezing breath like that of an old man with a hole in his windpipe. He heard a low steady dragging sound and a sniff. The tunnel was now carrying noise with a frightening clarity.

It was time. Siri got to his feet and walked slowly back toward the last room. Since he'd entered the tunnel, he'd counted the distances in paces. It was forty back to the deep well. At thirty-eight, he'd stop and proceed carefully until he found the drop. But as he walked, the sounds grew even louder behind him. He was tempted to run, but he knew the limitations of his lungs.

Then, one new sound made him stop completely. It was brief but unmistakable: it was the sob of a woman. He listened for a repeat of it, but heard nothing but the snarls and ever-loud howling. Could it have been . . . ?

He reached the end of his count and began to tread carefully, bent over using his iron as a walking stick. The step was further than he'd calculated: annoyingly further. By the time he finally reached it, his breathing was strained again, but there was no chance to rest. He stepped carelessly down into the pit and crunched some of the debris under his foot.

The sounds behind him immediately stopped, and he froze in position. There was the standoff: Siri fighting for breath, half up, half down, not daring to make another sound. And there was the dilemma: was the creature also frozen, listening for other sounds, or was it already running silently in his direction? If the latter were true, it could be on him at any second.

He looked back over his shoulder, fearing the worst.

"Breathe, Siri."

The view there should have been the same black tar he'd stared into since he arrived. He shouldn't have been able to see a thing, but for some reason, deep, deep at the end of his tunnel, there was a gray speck. It hadn't been there when he'd walked in that direction a while earlier.

It hadn't occurred to him for a second that the creature might need artificial light. Something had always made him believe it could find its way through the maze in darkness, using its instincts. But if it were part human, part Mr. Seua, perhaps it needed to use a lamp to see its way. Perhaps the distant grayness was the reflection from that light source. And perhaps that could be his one chance.

There came an almighty howl that echoed along the walls and passed Siri in a gust. The creature was on the move again, and Siri could indeed see that the gray shadow shimmered in time with the footsteps. He sighed with temporary relief.

Once again he waded through the matter in the pit, skating his shoes so as not to make undue sound. He skirted the perimeter of the room on one side, tapping the wall with his iron. He passed two corners. He found no other exit. He arrived at the opposite tunnel with time running out and inspected the other side of the room with new urgency. His premise was mistaken. The room had one entrance and one exit and no alternatives. His only hope was the pit.

Light, like a very distant sunrise, was beginning to filter down the tunnel. With a lamp, Seua would see him soon enough if he stayed in the room. But the creature might not think to look down below the lip of the step. Siri carefully cleared a space by the aperture through which the creature would arrive. He was a little off to the right, so he wouldn't be trodden on when it stepped down. He would have very little time to act.

There were two possibilities. If the creature's destination lay beyond this room, he would stay hidden and let it go. If its goal were the room itself, he wouldn't know until it had stepped down to where he was. He would eventually be discovered. But there might just be a few seconds in which to attack the creature, to spring at it from behind and hit it with the iron bar.

He knew he wouldn't be allowed more than one thwack, so he would have to be deadly accurate. It would need every last gram of Siri's strength. So he lay down against the step, practiced his meditation, and slowed his heartbeat to gather his resources for that one attack. And as more light filtered into the room, he could make out the carcasses of small creatures in varying stages of decay a foot deep all around him.

"Breathe, Siri."

Events that until that moment had been happening so fast, suddenly slowed as if time were stalling. The tunnel must have been longer than Siri had anticipated. The approaching sounds continued but the doctor felt as if he'd been lying there for an age. He had the opportunity to think about Yeh Ming and wondered why the old sage had failed to send warnings of this danger.

If ever his temple—he, Siri—were under threat, it was now. A terrible feeling of guilt came over Siri. Despite all the careful planning that had gone into his choice as host to the grand old shaman, he'd let him down. He'd knowingly put himself into a life-threatening sit—

Suddenly the creature was there. The beam of a flashlight dazzled directly into the room from just behind the step. From where he lay squashed tight against the dirt wall, Siri couldn't see who was holding it, but the sound of snarling was almost directly above him. Only a wedge of black shadow kept the doctor from sight.

His heart beat so loudly, he felt sure it could be heard. He breathed silently to a rhythm he'd set himself and gripped the iron bar tightly in his fist.

What happened next wouldn't be fully explained for a very long time. There were two halves to the mystery—one to baffle his hearing, one his sight—that wouldn't ever completely fit together. The sounds came first.

They began with footsteps shifting away from the step and the continued sound of dragging. There was one final howl. Then, from a point way beyond, came three incongruous sounds one after the other. First was the clucking of a chicken. Unlike all the other sounds, it didn't resonate around the room.

There followed two heavy thumps and a loud crack.

Finally came the scream of a woman.

Then there was silence.

When he heard the scream, Siri abandoned all caution and clambered noisily to his hands and knees. But before he could hoist himself into a position to see over the step, the light from the flashlight went out.

It was a darkness more profound and a silence more total than he'd ever encountered in his life, because it followed directly on the heels of chaos. He had no idea what he'd just heard or what to expect. He couldn't get the eerie scream from his mind.

"Dtui?" he shouted.

His voice exploded in the new silence like thunder.

"Dtui? Is that you? . . . It's Siri."

There was no reply.

If the creature were there in that blackness, Siri was now exposed. But there was no calling back his voice. There was no turning around. Something awful had just happened, and he needed to know what it was.

He climbed the step and shuffled forward, expecting his feet to find evidence of some horrific scene. His left foot kicked against something that rolled away. He knew it had to be the flashlight. He took a step forward and fumbled around in front of him on the packed earth. But his hand came to rest in something warm and wet and sticky like molasses.

He pulled away and took as deep a breath as he could. He knew what he'd found. But this was no time to become squeamish. He continued to sweep his palms back and forth until he made contact with the flashlight. He grabbed it, located the switch and, with his heart in his mouth, clicked it on.

Nothing happened.

"Please, Buddha, don't say the bulb's gone."

He tapped the flashlight and shook it and tried the switch again.

Still nothing.

From a little way ahead of him, no more than a yard, there came a breath. He rattled the battery frantically, shook the flashlight again, smacked it harder against his palm.

Another breath came from the dark.

He took one breath of his own, concentrated, screwed the head of the flashlight tight, and tried the switch one more time.

The tunnel lit up like a theater and, looking around him upon its stage, he saw the most impossible, the most extraordinary scene.

The Man Who Ripped Off His Own Head

Dtui awoke face-down. The scent of Breeze laundry detergent filled her nostrils. Her other senses were slower to come around. A fluffy white kitten lay some two feet from her head. It had no visible legs or face.

She couldn't feel her own tongue in her mouth, so she knew the medication was strong. She didn't want to begin to imagine what pain it was covering or what parts she might be missing. She just basked for a minute or two in the state of being alive.

The side of her face felt flat against the pillow, as if it had been there for an eternity. But no amount of willpower would convince her head to change its position. So she looked sideways at the familiar room through eyes gummy with the emissions of sleep.

There was nothing to distinguish one of Mahosot's private rooms from another. They all had the same Wattay blue walls, one traditional Lao print of an elephant, a year-old Thai plowing calendar, and a window too high up to see out of. She'd spent many hours in these rooms before her morgue career, but never in a bed. She felt a little like royalty—very sore, immobile royalty.

The kitten stirred. Growing out of its bottom were a small nose, a mouth, and two very green eyes that seemed to take some time to realize Dtui was staring back.

"Dtui?"

"Hello."

She sounded like a crocodile.

Siri was truly delighted. His neck was stiff from falling asleep during his watch again, but he clapped his hands and touched her numb cheek with the tips of his fingers. His smile made her feel important.

"Well, it's about time," he said. "How do you feel?"

"I don't."

Siri reached down below the sheet.

"Hey. What are you doing down there?"

She tried to smile but dribbled instead. Siri retrieved her arm and took her pulse.

"You have no more secrets from me, I'm afraid, Nurse Dtui."

Pleased with the pulse count, he took a tissue from the roll and wiped her mouth and eyes.

"Why am I face-down?"

"Most of your wounds are on your back. Do you remember what happened?"

In fact she did. Most of it remained clear in her mind, although she would have preferred otherwise.

"I was dragged, and. . . ."

"And beaten."

"Dr. Siri?"

"Yes?"

"Did he . . . mess with me?"

"No. Not at all."

"That's good."

She may have managed a smile. Siri may still have been talking. But she was soon unconscious again.

She swooned back into the room several more times that day. On one occasion, a big grinning Mr. Geung was leaning over her, encouraging her to stay awake, saying something about disinfectant prices.

On another, she may have been entertaining a flock of white-uniformed nursing students.

One more time, Civilai sat reading a report, making pencil notes in the margins.

The last time, it was dark but for a covered lamp on the table beside her. Siri slept in the corner of the room on an unlikely hospital reclining deck chair. She'd used up all her sleep, so had nothing to occupy her time other than reliving her demon. Now was the moment when she could either box him away in a dusty corner of her psyche and let him rattle from time to time, or exorcise him and let herself get on with life.

The night ticked on painfully slowly. The doctor slept with a crafty smile on his lips. She wondered what moment he was reliving in his dream, what happy time was revisiting him from the past. But she needed him awake.

"Dr. Siri. Dr. Siri."

The poor man was disoriented. He'd had a full day at the morgue: an accidental double shooting at the army training ground. Half-awake, he remembered where he was, hurried over to Dtui and took her wrist.

"You're doing very well," he said, swaying slightly.

"Will I live?"

"A lot longer than me. You really are an amazingly resilient young thing."

"Siri, what's happened to my mom?"

He blushed. "Ah, yes. That."

"Doc?"

"Well, she's moved in with me."

"You don't waste any time, do you? Is she okay?"

"She's fine now. She's very relieved that you pulled through."

"How bad was I?"

"The first three days, we weren't sure you'd make it."

"Damn."

"You'd lost a lot of blood."

"I've been here longer than three days?"

"Dtui, it's April 10th. You've been here well over three weeks. It's almost Lao New Year."

"God, how am I ever going to afford . . . ? I can't pay for all this and Ma, and. . . ."

He smiled and shook his head.

"No. Don't worry about it. You wouldn't believe how well things have worked out on that front. I'll tell you all about it later. The bills are taken care of."

Siri spent some time looking at Dtui's wounds and doing a few basic tests.

"Doc, I'm sorry I woke you up. I wanted to talk about it."

"We will."

"No, I mean now. I need to verbalize it. I really think the sooner I get it all out of my system, the better."

"It could be quite draining. Are you sure you're strong enough?"

"I'm wide awake and pumping."

"Then talk away. I can't tell you how much I've been looking forward to solving this last little mystery. It's been driving me nutty."

He pulled over the straight-back chair from the desk and sat beside her with his hand on hers.

"Uncle Civilai told me about the tunnels."

"What made you think of looking underground?"

"There's this old lady at the slum. People call her a witch 'cause she knows all about these old traditions and uses herbal potions. I went to ask her about the weretiger. She told me about the caves and the holes down into the other world. As no witnesses had come forward to say they'd seen the creature, it seemed logical that it was in hiding. But there aren't that many places above ground you can hide in a city like Vientiane.

"I didn't plan to go down there and be some Wonder Woman character, honestly I didn't. I hate confined spaces. Even our room at the shanty gives me the willies. I just went down to take a look, really. I didn't have any evidence, you see? I had nothing to prove he was down there. So I went to see if it was likely, or even possible. I opened the slab and went down to the bottom of the ladder and flashed my light down the tunnel. I called out, 'Anyone down here?'

"There was no answer. I didn't hear any sounds. There was no way in Hades I was about to go down that tunnel. So I was just climbing back up the ladder when this big shadow comes over me and bang, something smashes me over the head.

"I came to and he's got my flashlight and he's dragging me through the tunnel by the wrist just like I don't weigh anything. I was dizzy, but I struggled and screamed and he gave me another thump with the butt of the flashlight. He was incredibly strong. It was a sort of superhuman strength."

"You knew who it was straight away?"

"Dr. Vansana had described Mr. Seua to me. The physical description was the same, but this wasn't the sociable, likable fellow the doctor knew from Don Thao: this was a maniac. I tried to talk to him, calm him down, but I knew something had snapped.

"He left me somewhere in the tunnel and went off with the light. That was worse than the violence: the dark. Siri, I've never been so scared. I was drowsy from the blow and bloody from all the dragging. And it was so completely black, I was just left with my thoughts."

"I know exactly how you felt."

"He came back once or twice with stray dog carcasses and squirrels. He'd sit in front of me in the lamplight and rip them apart with his teeth and eat them raw. I've seen some disgusting things in my life, but that beat 'em all.

"Even then, I didn't know what to expect. I knew about the victims and the tooth marks. But he was a man, a big powerful man but still a man. I supposed at some stage he'd turn into a weretiger once his blood tank was full, and I'd be his next victim. I was convinced when the moon rose, I'd get to witness the change."

Siri took a tissue from the roll and dabbed at the tears that streamed down her face into the pillow.

"Thanks. I had my watch then and I kept thinking about the moon. I knew if I had any chance to escape, it would have to be before midnight. When he was with me he'd beat me, slap me cruelly, for no reason. I was already very weak but I knew there'd only be one chance. He went off once with the light and I mustered all my strength and headed into the blackness in the opposite direction. I believe my nerves had shut off the pain by then. I could barely feel my legs but fear drove me on.

"I don't know how long I staggered. There was nowhere to hide. I didn't know where I was going, but I prayed I'd come to a way out. Then there was a light. I was so happy that, in my feverous state, I believed I'd been rescued. I looked through the beam, and there was Seua's bloodied mouth snarling at me.

"That was the beating that finished me off. I only remember one more thing after that, waking up to an unbelievable sight. Even now I'm not sure whether I dreamed it, but it seemed so real."

"Describe it to me in detail."

"Well, the flashlight was on the ground shining directly at Seua. He'd changed since I'd last seen him. Not the metamorphosis type of change, I mean he'd changed his clothes. I realized what had happened. There was no weretiger, not in the physical sense, but he had this secret identity he could change into.

"He had this fur. Who knows what type of animal—or animals—it was from. It was tied around his body with ropes. It was on his arms and legs too. And there was a hood. That was made of fur as well, black fur with eyeholes cut out of it. He was pretty well covered, but I could tell it was him from the way he moved.

"On the back of his left hand, strapped there, was a paw. I assumed it was a real animal paw with the claws extended over his fingers. If he'd clenched his fist it would have made a frightening weapon. I can't believe how clear that all was, how much I remember from those few seconds. On the ground at his feet was the jawbone of another animal, or the same animal. The teeth were really sharp. I got the feeling he'd dropped it. I don't know how it fitted in with the rest of the costume at all.

"I became fixated with whatever it was that was happening to Seua. It was incredible. Something had certainly got into him, or into his hood. He was ripping at it with both hands in panic as if some insect or rat or something had crawled inside it. He pulled it off and the claw accidentally raked over his face. It left this deep fast-bleeding wound across his eye.

"But removing the hood didn't seem to get rid of the problem, Doc. It even made it worse. He was slapping at his head like whatever had been in his hood was now inside his skull. I was amazed. He took a run, full speed and head first, at the side of the tunnel. Just like that. As if it was someone else's head he was throwing at the wall. It didn't work. He smashed his head again, then grabbed his ears.

"Dr. Siri, it was like he was trying to wrestle his own head off his shoulders. And the Lord Buddha protect me if he didn't do it. He stood there over me, wrenched at his head with both hands, and snapped his own neck. He almost pulled it clean off. It just flopped down like a puppet's.

"I screamed. I remember that much. Then I was out of it. I was swirling around in nightmare-land till I woke up today and saw your fluffy white head on my bed."

"That was the day before yesterday."

"I'm not surprised."

All the while, Siri had been mopping up both their tears with a hand towel. Now, as soon as she was done with her story, the tears stopped and she smiled. She wasn't purged of her demon, but he would be easier to control now.

"All this time, I've been worried I was wrong with the autopsy," Siri said. "It didn't make any sense. Who, in any state of mind, would be able to twist off his own head? I had to assume you or some other person had done it. But there was no evidence on his body that he'd been in a fight.

"The scratches were clearly from his weapon. The blood on his face matched that on the wall. He died from a broken neck, and I could convince nobody, not even myself, that he was the one who did it."

"Well, he did, Doc. I'm a sorry witness to that. Did you get anything else at the autopsy?"

"The claw and the jaw bone were both from a real tiger, and they match the marks we copied from the bodies. God knows where he got them. He'd set up this complicated grip on the jaw so he could use it like a glove puppet. He'd wear it on his hand and he could really bite with it. It must have been confusing for him that he didn't really materialize into the weretiger he believed he was.

"The fur was one more example of how much time went into this secret identity you mentioned. It was sewn together painstakingly from the pelts of all those animals I found in the pit: dogs, cats, possums, anything he could lay his hands on. He must have spent all the time between his release and the full moon to set it up.

"There were nodule growths on his brain: small tumors. I'm ashamed to say they meant nothing to me. It's all a bit beyond my humble field of expertise. I have no idea what they mean, but I'm not counting out one theory I heard that night. There might be a connection between the moon's energy when it's full and the electrical impulses in the brain. It could explain the rapid change in his personality.

"I've taken samples of everything. When you go to Russia,

you can take them with you, find yourself a good-looking young forensic scientist, and follow up on this for your thesis."

"Yes. Dream On, I and II."

"Not necessarily. The next exams are at the end of May. Given what you've done already, I don't see why you shouldn't get through those easily enough."

"They wouldn't even let me sit."

"Your name's already on the roster."

"How the hell did you swing that?"

"They're desperate for people with a basic grasp of Russian."

"How did you know . . . ? Has my mom been engaging in pillow talk?"

"Don't be vulgar, girl. Nothing improper is going on between your mother and me . . . or Mr. Inthanet."

"Jesus, is he still here?"

"I can't get him to go home. But I must say, my house is a lot more palatable with other people in it. I don't feel quite so much like a dowager duchess in her castle. The old fellow's stepping out with my next-door neighbor."

"Not the creepy guy from Oudom Xay?"

"No. Dear Mr. Soth moved out under mysterious circumstances. I came home one evening to find him and his family and all their furniture gone. I mean the other neighbor, my own Miss Vong."

"Vong and Inthanet? You must be joking."

"Not at all. They appear to be getting along very nicely, and it does keep her out of my hair."

"Are they, you know, performing together?"

"Dtui. No. It's all very proper. They go for motorbike rides down to the river, hold hands listening to her traditional tapes in the back garden."

"How sweet."

"I think it was all a bit too sickening for my dog."

"Saloop?"

"He's left home."

"I thought you two were inseparable."

"Obviously not. I think he's found himself a—"

"Siri."

"What is it?"

He hurried across to check her pipes and wires.

"I saw him. I saw Saloop."

"Where?"

"That day. That day in the tunnel when I came around. It completely went out of my head till you mentioned him. He was just sitting, watching Seua run amok."

"You sure you didn't add him later, in your dreams?"

"No. 'Cause when I saw him, I remember wondering whether you were around, too. I guessed you'd come looking and brought Saloop with you."

"He wasn't with me."

"And you didn't see him?"

"No. When I got the flashlight working, I saw the aftermath of the scene you just described, but with one addition. There was an old lady—I mean the spirit of the same old lady that came to our office often when you two had gone home."

"You forgot to mention that."

"Didn't want to spook anyone. Well, she was there, or *it* was there, standing over Seua's body. I went to do what I could for you, and she vanished. But Saloop; I have no idea how he found his way into the tunnels. I've been seeing him in some odd places lately, but he's definitely gone back to his old street life. He doesn't even have the manners to come and visit from time to time."

"Perhaps he's afraid of all those house guests, Siri, and he'll come home when they've gone. Doc?"

"Yes?"

"Thanks."

"For?"

"Everything. Thanks for coming to look for me that day. Thanks for taking care of Mom. Thanks for being here now. I owe you big-time."

"You can pay me back by passing those exams."

"Just as well you don't want it in cash. What was the secret about paying the bills here you couldn't tell me?"

"Dtui, sweetheart, it's three-thirty in the morning and I have a kidney to dissect at eight. You don't suppose I could have a little sleep before then, do you? Even if you aren't tired, I'm exhausted."

"Sorry. You're right. Go get some sleep."

"You need anything?"

She thought about spending the rest of her life with a triangular face.

"A new perspective? You couldn't flip my face, could you?"

"I don't see why not."

He took her chin in one hand and her forehead in the other and gently dragged her nose across the pillow to face the other wall. It gave her a brief preview of the pain she'd be enjoying over the next week. Siri sighed and creaked back into his chair.

"G'night, Dtui."

"G'night, Doc."

"Oh, Doc?"

"Yeah?"

"Is it still hot outside?"

"Damned hot."

April New Year

Vientiane was preparing for New Year on the 14th with its usual verve. Houses had to be cleaned, repairs made, old scores forgiven. It was customary to begin the new year in a state of physical and moral cleanliness.

March and early April had been the hottest on record, and a lot of people had forgotten what rain felt like. Excluding the Government, everyone was looking forward to a few days of water tossing, and hosing down, and walking around in shorts and rubber sandals. *Songkran* was Laos's most joyous and uninhibited calendar event.

All the splashing generally got Mother Nature in the mood too, and she'd join in with some generous pre-season rainstorms to begin the long process of slaking the thirst of the land. But if old Mother Nature had been in the meeting at the Interior Ministry on the eleventh, she'd probably have become as hotheaded as Civilai.

He stormed out after the final vote with his glasses steamed up and his two aides scuttling along after him.

"Fools," was all he had to say.

It was Sunday. Inthanet, with the invaluable aid of his lovely assistant, Miss Vong, was making the final preparations for his big show. From his vantage point on the hammock in the back yard, Siri couldn't help noticing the red flushes on their collective cheeks. Either sewing hems on royal capes was hot work, or they'd been up to something. Siri didn't relish getting a mental picture of what that may have been, but he was pleased that Miss Vong finally had a little romance in her life.

Manoluk lay sleeping on the cot on the veranda. One over-worked fan whirled at her feet at the end of a daisy chain of extension cords that brought it out to the garden. Another chain led to the living room, where a second fan swept back and forth drying the new paint faces of a lineup of delighted puppets. A third fan puffed at the ruddy cheeks of the lovers in the back room. The radio played northern flute music live from the army studio. The refrigerator made ice for the lemon tea. The rice cooker prepared lunch.

The drain on the national electric grid from Siri's house alone was enormous. He expected a raid at any second. So when the bell rang from the front gate—a bell that only strangers used—he knew the jig was up.

"Visitor," Miss Vong called out.

"So I gathered," Siri agreed. "I don't suppose you'd like to go and see who it is, would you?"

"I'm threading."

"Of course you are."

The old Miss Vong would have been at the fence with her binoculars and notepad at the first footfall on the front path. Now she didn't care. Siri reluctantly climbed down from the hammock and shuffled stiffly through the house. The bell had rung with great urgency twice more before he reached the front.

"Patience, patience," he said, and creaked open the gate that was neither locked nor latched.

To his amazement, Mrs. Fah, the wife of his old neighbor, Soth, stood a few paces back from the gate. She'd been crying and was shaking violently.

"Mrs. Fah. What's wrong?"

"Dr. Siri, can you come with me, please?"

These were more words than they'd exchanged in all the time they'd lived next door to one another.

"What is it?"

"My husband is dying, and he says it's your fault."

Siri rode his motorcycle with Mrs. Fah on the back, holding his bag. She gave directions, and he was interested to see that the neighbors had moved about a mile from their old house to a similar suburb. The woman insisted on getting off the bike long before the house came into view and walking ahead, lest her husband see her. In fact, the new house was almost identical to the one they'd left in such a hurry. It was all most peculiar.

Mrs. Fah hadn't given Siri any details of her husband's ailment, so he didn't know what to expect. He parked in the street and followed the wife through the opulent house to the bedroom. The huge king-size bed contained a remarkably shriveled Mr. Soth at its center. His skin was gray, and his cheekbones stood out on his face.

"Mr. Soth, what's happened to you?"

The man opened his eyes slowly and glared at Siri.

"As you see, Doctor, I've been struck down."

"By what?"

He reached out for Soth's wrist but the man pulled away.

"I don't need your medicine. I can afford a dozen real doctors. None of them have helped."

"I don't understand. What caused this?"

Soth looked beyond Siri.

"That."

Siri turned his head and was stunned to see a trim version of Saloop lying in the corner of the room with his head on one paw.

"Saloop? Well, I'll be. So this is where you got to. How are you, boy?"

Soth's eyes grew wide. "So you can see it."

"Of course I can."

"Of course? My wife can't. The kids can't. Nobody else can see the damned thing but me. I've had three fortune-tellers here telling me it doesn't exist."

Siri stared at Saloop, who showed no sign of recognizing his old master. His eyes were glazed and red like cocktail cherries. His fur was dull. His left ear seemed to sit lower on his head than his right. There was no movement but for the irregular rise and fall of its breath. Siri was overcome with a sudden pang of sadness.

What he saw there was not his dog; it was the malevolent spirit of an animal that had suffered an unnatural death.

"It's dead," Soth said, and a tear appeared in the corner of his eye.

"Why's he here?"

"It's here to haunt me. It won't rest till it sees me on my pyre. It won't let me eat or sleep. It plans to stay here until I rot away."

"But why?"

"Why? Why? Because I killed it, that's why."

"You killed my dog?"

"Yes, but because of you. Because you tried to make a fool of me. You didn't leave me with any choice. I lured it into my yard and brained it with a shovel. It was to get back at you. This is all your fault."

"The dog didn't have anything to do with you or me."

"It was your dog. I knew you liked it. It was just revenge."

"But of course he's not going to see a connection. Only man would hurt a third party to get revenge on someone who'd wronged him. It's against nature. If your grievance was with me, you should have settled your debt with me directly. The dog's spirit doesn't know why you hate it."

"It's you I hate. This was all your fault. The bloody dog drove me out of my house, then followed me here. I can't shake it off. You make it go away."

"I can't do that."

"Can't? Look at me, Siri. Look what state I'm in. You want my death on your conscience forever? Call off your dog."

"No. I mean it isn't for me to do. You have to beg forgiveness from the spirit of the dog for what you did."

"Huh? I'm not asking a damned dog for forgiveness. What do you think I am?"

Siri looked at the man, still arrogant even at the threshold of death. He showed no remorse. The only person who could remove this curse was Soth himself, but to do that he had to accept responsibility.

"Mr. Soth, I'm going to be perfectly frank with you. There's only one way for you to save yourself, but it is possible. You need to stop shifting the blame for all this onto me. You have to perform a *basee* ceremony and truly believe that you and you alone have caused this. You have to ask the spirit of the dog to forgive you. No one else can remove this burden."

"So you're refusing?"

"No. I'm telling you what to do. I'm giving you a way out."

"I curse you for this, Siri. I curse you a hundred times."

Siri closed his bag and walked to the door. He looked down at Soth.

"You're in exalted company on that front, Mr. Soth. Don't forget what I said. It's all up to you."

Soth spat in the doctor's direction.

In the living room, he reported his warning to Mrs. Fah and gave her the same instructions.

"He'll never do it," she said.

"If he doesn't, he won't survive this."

"No? Good riddance."

Her honesty shocked but didn't actually surprise him. He'd heard how the husband talked to the wife. He'd seen her kept as a slave in his house. She was glad this was happening, and once Siri confirmed that her husband wouldn't make it, she'd finally had the courage to speak her mind.

"If you need any help," Siri said, "you know where I live. I'm serious."

On the short ride home, Siri tried to put his emotions into some kind of order. He didn't feel guilt at this haunting. He was sad his dog had died, but proud the animal had gone after the bastard. It's what he would have done. As for Soth, this was the backlash of Yin to punish him for his years of Yang. He couldn't fight that. It comes to everyone, either in this life or in the next. He was glad to see that even in times of confusion such as these, the laws of *I Ching* were still in order.

No Spontaneous Fun—by Order

The sign at the back of the stage was written in stylish letters on a white banner.

BENEFIT SHOW FOR THE NURSES' MEDICAL FUND

For everyone on the Medical School football field that evening, this was the undisputed highlight of the *Songkran* celebrations. There had been so few events to cheer.

Politburo Directive 873 had basically put an end to spontaneous celebrations. New Year water throwing had only been allowed at designated spots under the watchful eye of PL representatives. There had been arrests of those who ignored the directive, and in places where anarchy reigned in large numbers, long lists of names were submitted to the authorities.

Due to the prolonged drought, water was throwable only from 2 P.M. to 5 P.M. and had to be taken from natural sources such as ponds and rivers. Water from the public supply was off limits under threat of a nine-thousand-*kip* fine. Most musician and comedian concerts had been cancelled, and the giving of alms to monks in the morning had been kept very low key. There were to be no outward signs of extravagance.

So, for people living in and near the downtown area, this show was pretty much it, and if it hadn't been for Siri, they wouldn't even have had this. In the late afternoon, the Medical

School football team had won the annual grudge match against the Law School, 13–8. They then started to set the field up for the entertainment.

Chairs for VIPs were laid out in twenty rows in front of a stage. These were cordoned off from the standing public by lengths of pink nylon string tied to bamboo posts. The team's supporters were all made to leave the field and re-enter, this time paying their fifty *kip*. All proceeds were to go to the Nurses' Fund.

By 6:30, most of the VIP chairs were full and the field was crammed with onlookers mumbling with excitement. Children and particularly short people were hustled good-naturedly to the front of the standing gallery, and people at the back stood on boxes and bricks.

In the sixth row of the VIP chairs sat Civilai, Mr. Geung, and Siri, in that order. They watched as the most "I" of the VIPs arrived fashionably late. The same people who had banned festivals and public gatherings were excitedly taking their seats in front of them, nodding and waving as if they'd organized this show themselves.

Civilai had maintained a foul mood for three days now. He'd spent much of his life as a frustrated Nostradamus. He knew what benefits or consequences there would be from decisions made or policy introduced at any given time. He really knew. But he'd rarely been able to convince the majority. No matter how often he'd been proven right, they still saw him as a noisy reactionary cog in the revolutionary machine.

The festival directive, he knew would be a disaster. The people were suffering. They'd tightened their belts at the behest of the new regime. They'd pooled their scant resources and given up their humble luxuries. And what reward did they get for their unselfishness? Zilch. They needed festivals and concerts and happy days now and then in order to forget their frustrations.

But the Party saw these gatherings as potential boiling pots of political unrest. They were afraid of young people, with the same fire that had once burned in their own breasts, raging through the village festivals and leading to a popular uprising. After eighteen months in power, paranoia had become a national symptom.

The first test would come in May. The popular rocket festival had been banned completely. "Too many people; too much gunpowder," they'd said at the meeting. Civilai argued until he was no longer red in the face that you couldn't just erase a festival that had been part of the culture for hundreds of years. The rocket festival was a fertility rite. It appeased the gods of the harvest and begged them to bring the rainy season. What would happen if the festival were banned and the rains didn't start on time? What would the people think of their new regime then?

They scolded Civilai for his superstitious ways and voted him down—again.

"They'll be sorry," Civilai mumbled as the prime minister took his seat. "Look at those old fogies."

"They're all younger than you," Siri reminded him.

"Only in years, Siri. In mentality they've all got one foot in the grave."

"T . . . too . . . too bad Dtui can't be here t . . . to . . . to see this," Mr. Geung said, appropriately changing the subject. He sucked happily on his corn ice pole, a rare treat in those hard times. Civilai agreed.

"She'll be up and about in a week or so. She *should* be here, considering that all her medical bills are going to be covered by this little performance."

"And . . . and all the o . . . o . . . other nurses that get sick," Geung reminded him.

"It's a service the government should be offering, not you, Siri. We should—"

"Come on, older brother. Let's enjoy this, can we?" Siri urged. "Take off your grumpy hat and relax."

"Ha, grumpy hat." Geung found that a hilarious concept and laughed contagiously. Civilai and Siri and a dozen people around them caught it.

"All right," Civilai conceded. "I'll enjoy myself."

"Good."

"On the condition that you tell me how you swung this little con."

"Swung? Con? Civilai, this is a joint Ministry of Sport and Culture–Russian Embassy event. No swinging was involved. What do you mean?"

"Getting them both to agree to support your Nurses' Fund, for one thing. That had to involve some very sharp political maneuvering, Dr. Siri."

"Not really."

A Ukrainian man with a guitar climbed up on the stage, sat on a rickety stool, and proceeded to warm up the audience with American folk songs translated into Russian.

"Come on." Civilai leaned across Geung and spoke in a low voice. "How did you do it?"

Siri leaned over as well, but Geung found it all too funny, so he and Siri changed seats.

"You have to promise not to tell anyone."

"Who'd listen to me?"

"Okay. I blackmailed them."

"Who?"

"All of them. The ministry people, the Russians."

"Oh, come on."

"Really. The head of the archive department at DSIC was moonlighting at Tong Kankum market, selling fish during office hours. That, you have to agree, is against regulations. So he thought it would be a very socially aware thing to offer the proceeds of a concert to the sick nurses."

"In exchange for. . . ."

"My silence."

"Okay. That I can believe. But the Russians? What have you got that they want?"

"Well, it was Dtui, actually, who sparked my interest. When she went to see Ivanic, she said she saw this nocturnal panda they'd just smuggled in through customs. I'd never heard of an animal changing its sleep habits to suit the weather, so it got me suspicious. I checked with my spy at Wattay. There hadn't been any flights, direct or indirect, from China during the period they claimed the panda had arrived.

"So I tried a little bluff. You remember the bear at the Lan Xang that started all this fuss?"

"Yes."

"Everyone had believed it was too infirm to have made it out of the hotel compound without help. So I wondered what type of person might love animals enough, and have the resources, to rescue the poor old girl. The name of Ivanic popped up in my suspicious mind. What if he and his secret police friends did a raid to spring the bear and take her to the circus compound?"

"He didn't?"

"He would have needed a good cover story to explain the sudden appearance of a bear, especially as most of the armed forces were out hunting for it. That's when he came up with the Chinese panda alibi."

"How do you turn a Malay black into a panda?"

"Bleach, and enough shadows to make sure nobody gets too close. Once I'd come up with that little theory, it seemed more and more plausible. So I approached the Russian with it."

"Well done."

"Being a good Soviet Communist, he came straight to the point and asked me what I'd want to keep my mouth shut. So, here we are: circus day."

"Siri, apart from myself, you have to be the most devious old bastard I know."

He threw back his head and laughed, put his arm around his friend's neck and kissed him on the cheek.

"Get off."

"That's wonderful, really. It makes up for everything else. It honestly does. God, I love you."

He kissed him again.

Civilai giggled through the entire show. The big Lao girls in their underwear tumbled bravely and climbed into swaying towers of bodies. Three jugglers kept a lovely bunch of coconuts in the air for the longest time. A clown in ever-falling trousers brought excited howls and hoots from the huge crowd.

At halftime, a Lao orchestra came on the stage, and in front of them a smartly attired Mr. Inthanet and some Fine Arts students presented a play with the Royal Puppets. It was a magical moment, and when it was over the crowd truly believed they'd been honored to see it. The puppets got the loudest cheer of the night. They would return to their teak chest pumped with pride from a magnificent performance that would be talked about forever.

For the final act, a wagon covered in a black cloth was wheeled in front of the VIPs. Ivanic, in his leather thigh-high boots and a frilled pink shirt open to the navel, pranced down from the apron of the stage like the ham showman he was. He shouted some indecipherable words to the audience and grandly pulled back the cloth.

The glistening black puma, elegant and frightening under the glare of the spotlights, prowled back and forth in the small cage, growling at the huge audience. They first gasped at the sight of the magnificent creature, then applauded. With his arm twirling through the air and his deep incomprehensible voice enthralling the onlookers, Ivanic walked to one side of the cage. The puma charged at him. He charged back and the two stood eyeballing one another through the bars. Ivanic reached up and pulled a large metal pin from the side of the cage and the entire front flap dropped to the ground.

The sudden intake of breath almost sucked the performers into the audience. The creature looked to one side and tensed with excited apprehension. There was nothing now between it and the front row of the VIP seats but warm air and a sudden charge of anxiety. The old men tensed. Some stood and prepared to run. The bodyguards on either side reached for their pistols and took a step forward.

The puma froze. The audience froze.

"Eat 'em," shouted Civilai.

But before any eating could take place, Ivanic stepped bravely forward into the void 'twixt the drooling animal and the perspiring VIPs. With his back to the puma, he raised his right hand. There came a growl from behind him and the animal seemed to half squat, ready to spring. Some women screamed, but they were the ones too far to see the calm on Ivanic's face.

Slowly and reluctantly, the puma sat.

"Damn," Civilai said.

Ivanic raised his other hand, and the puma rose up in slow motion and paddled its claws through the air. There came a nervous round of applause from an audience afraid that a sudden noise might snap the animal out of its passivity.

The Russian coolly folded his arms and put down his head. The puma lay down and, still snarling, rolled onto its back. Then, calm as you like, Ivanic strolled over to the platform of the cage where the puma lay and sat beside it. He reached out his hand with its fake crowd-pleasing shake and patted the beast on the belly.

There was a huge cheer from the throng. The VIPs clapped politely but not with any confidence. The cage was, after all, still open. Ivanic spotted Siri in the sixth row and nodded. Siri, as delighted as everyone else, nodded back. It was, they all agreed, the most magnificent New Year show they'd ever seen.

A Brace of Epilogues

Siri was just leaving Hay Sok temple when he saw his nameless monk beside the exit. There he sat, quite unashamedly, on the back of a concrete lion beside the path where all the real monks could see him.

"I didn't expect to find you here," Siri said.

"And why not, Yeh Ming?"

"According to the abbot, you don't exist."

"Don't you see me, Yeh Ming? Don't you hear my voice?"

"I'm sure you exist, or existed as a person, but not as a monkat this temple at this time. I described your tattoos to him, and he swears there's no such monk as you at his temple."

"Perhaps nobody else noticed my tattoos."

"Perhaps nobody else noticed you."

"It's possible. I find that more and more people fail to see things that are right under their noses. Tell me, did you solve your weretiger mystery?"

"Parts of it. I'm still not satisfied. But at least he's dead."

"Then I don't see what there is to worry about."

"I don't know why he died."

"It sounds like it was his time."

"Yes. There's no doubt about that. But if he killed himself, he did so in a most awful and bizarre way."

"Describe it to me."

"He ripped his own head half off. I don't know what could possess a man to do such a thing."

"I imagine any number of things could have possessed him."

"For example?"

"I've seen such bizarre things before. Things even more horrible."

"You have? I can't imagine anything worse than ripping your own head off."

"Oh dear, yes. Imagine that you looked at the end of your leg and saw that a rat had eaten your foot. It was still there, about to gnaw its way up your shin. Wouldn't you do anything you could to shake that rat off?"

"Yes."

"Wouldn't you hit it with a hammer if you had one—cut it with a sword?"

"Yes."

"So all that's necessary is to convince you there's a rat on your leg. To a man who already has delusions that he's a weretiger, I wouldn't think it too difficult to convince him his head wasn't his own. He would certainly believe his head was a poison toadstool or a blowfish—"

"Or a chicken?"

"It's possible. He wasn't ripping off his head. He was fighting off the illusion that had been planted there."

"By whom?"

"Any one of a number of spirits. There are many watching over you. They're always with you."

"Are you one of them?"

The monk stood and smiled.

"Ah, no. I'm just an old monk."

"Then you wouldn't object to my shaking your hand, old monk."

"It isn't appropriate."

He turned and started to walk into the dark shadows of the temple moon trees. Siri called after him.

"There's an old woman. She has a penchant for betel nut. She was in the tunnel."

"I know her," the monk called back without turning round. "She wasn't one of my clients. I don't recognize her."

"You knew her, but you were too young to remember. She has more interest in keeping you alive than any of us."

"Who is she?"

The monk was just another shadow between the trees now.

"Even coroners have mothers, Yeh Ming. Even coroners."

The black Malay bear lay on her back and stretched her limbs like a well-fed housecat. She couldn't stop this feeling of bliss from spreading to her smiling mouth. She had at last experienced kindness and it was a marvelous feeling.

She had more food than she could eat in a lifetime. She had a new fashionable design on her fur. Her wounds and sores had been treated, and she'd felt love from humans—a species she'd only ever known as hostile.

She'd escaped from the truck on the second night of her rescue when it stopped at the gate of Silver City. They were transferring her from a room at the Soviet clinic where her maladies were treated. She believed she must have been on her way to the abattoir. Her instinct told her to take advantage of this comparative freedom and seek out the shaman. It told her he was close by. She followed her nose to his house and lay in wait in the lot behind his yard.

Yeh Ming lived inside an old man. When the host slept, the bear asked the shaman for help. He allowed her to share thoughts for a time with her ancestors. He told her not to fear these new events in her life. She'd suffered so much unfortunate karma already, what remained could only be good. Her next life would be wonderful. She should seek out the people who had taken her from the hotel.

She thanked him and went to search for the gates of Silver City. It took her the longest time to find them. She was used up.

Her natural senses were draining away. She wouldn't see out this hot season, but her last months would be the happiest she'd known.

She lay on her back there in the large cage, took hold of a bunch of ladyfinger bananas in both paws, squeezed them like a concertina player, and sucked out the delicious fruit.

Colin Cotterill was born in London in 1952. He has taught in Australia, the United States, and Japan, and has lived in Thailand on the Burmese border, and in Laos. He lives in Chiang Mai, in northern Thailand. Colin Cotterill's website can be found at www.colincotterill.com.